BARBARIANS OF THE BEYOND

Spatterlight
Amstelveen 2021

BARBARIANS OF THE BEYOND

Matthew Hughes

A novel set in Jack Vance's Demon Princes universe

Published by Spatterlight, Amstelveen 2021

Cover art by Tiziano Cremonini

ISBN 978-1-61947-405-5

www.spatterlight.nl

BARBARIANS OF THE BEYOND

Prologue

In the late fifteenth century (New Reckoning), some three hundred families left Earth, heart of the interplanetary civilization of the Oikumene, for a sparsely settled world, Providence, in the largely lawless Beyond. Led by a utopia-inclined minor aristocrat, they established a farming colony in a place they called Mount Pleasant. These were hard-working folk, most of them of an independent character, and their community prospered. A small town grew up at the center of the colony, providing the farmers with whatever goods and services they could not produce for themselves. The town and its surrounding farms eventually came to support a population of more than five thousand.

Providence was one of many worlds in the Beyond whose inhabitants paid forced tribute to five master criminals of the Beyond: Attel Malagate, Kokor Hekkus, Viole Falushe, Lens Larque, and Howard Alan Treesong—the so-called Demon Princes. Once the colony was well established, the Demon Princes' collectors came to Mount Pleasant to inform the newcomers of their obligations. But the colonists would not pay, neither in funds nor in kind—especially since "kind" to the criminals meant human slaves. The Demon Princes decided to make an example of Mount Pleasant, while at the same time deriving profit from the atrocity by staging a raid on the colony.

In 1499, their ships descended upon Mount Pleasant, disgorging a surge of heavily armed pirates. The colonists who resisted were massacred. Those who surrendered were herded into the pirates' holds and carried off to the slave markets of the Beyond. None ever returned to Mount Pleasant.

The only survivors were a few colonists who had been out of town during the raid. Two of these were Rolf Gersen and his grandson, Kirth. They left Providence soon after for Earth and other worlds of the Oikumene, never to return. Mount Pleasant became a ghost town, standing empty for years, until a sect of religious enthusiasts whose neighbors had found them troublesome left their home world of Tantamount in the Oikumene and came to occupy the abandoned steadings and business premises.

No one knew what became of their stolen predecessors, until one day...

Chapter One

When the tramp freighter *Festerlein* touched down at the spaceport at Hambledon, on the world Providence, Morwen Sabine was no more than three paces from the forward cargo hatch, her ditty bag in hand. The moment the hatch cycled open to admit the health inspector and her team, Morwen squeezed past them with a soft-voiced, "Excuse," and headed quickly for the embarkation shed. Here she showed her spacer's card to an uninterested official in a wrinkled uniform who glanced at it only long enough to see that her face matched the image thereon, before waving her through the entry chicane.

The card said Morwen's name was Porfiria Ardcashin, an identity she had acquired a year previously, along with a false resume of ships on which she had supposedly served, for an appreciable number of Standard Value Units on Cafferty's Reach, a world deep in the Beyond — where cash in their pockets meant more to most people than regulations written in some functionary's book. Since then, Morwen's abilities as a fast learner had led her to accumulate some of the spacer's skills, but most of her time on the *Festerlein* had been spent in the galley, with brief stints as a cargo roustabout when the freighter put into this or that port.

But now, after so many stops on so many worlds, she had finally landed on Providence, an agricultural backwater an appreciable distance beyond the Pale that separated the civilized worlds of the Oikumene from the lawless Beyond. She passed through the rudimentary terminal building, her typical spacer's two-piece costume of dark blue and gray rendering her almost unnoticeable, then stepped out onto the surface of the world that should have been her own. The yellow sun was two handsbreadths above distant hills, her ultimate destination, making this late afternoon, local time.

The terminal had smelled like all such facilities, a mixture of fuels, disinfectants, and dust, but now she took her first inhalation of Providence's air. Every world had its own characteristic odor. Immediately, she sensed a mix of scents: a sweet headiness underlaid by a faint sulfury tang and a whiff of the pines brought by the original settlers from Earth. Not an unpleasant combination, but even if it had been, by tomorrow the smell would have become unnoticeable, as her senses became inured to it.

She crossed an expanse of pavement on which several ground vehicles were parked, moving quickly toward a carryall that was backing out of a space. As she reached it, it stopped and turned its front wheels toward the road that connected the spaceport to the city of Hambledon. Morwen rapped on the driver's window. He pushed it down and stared a question at her, a sandy-haired man with watery blue eyes set in a face that had not seen many hardships.

"Any chance of a lift?" she said.

"Where are you going?"

"Right now, to find a place to stay."

"And after?"

"A town called Mount Pleasant," Morwen said.

The man considered her statement as if it might hold some minor mystery, then his face cleared as he accepted it as merely a plain stating of facts. He said, "It's not called that anymore. The name for several years has been New Dispensation."

"Oh," said Morwen.

"There's a hotel not far from there. It's as close as I come to New Diss on this run. I can drop you off there."

"That would suit me," Morwen said. She went around the front of the vehicle and got in the passenger side, her ditty bag between her feet. The driver did things with the controls and they drove away.

Morwen shifted in her seat to see the rearview screen, found no one exiting the port terminal after her. She saw the driver glance her way and his gaze drop to where the cuff of her right sleeve had ridden up, exposing some of the tattoo on her inner forearm. She tugged the cloth down and stared ahead.

The man said something that sounded like nonsense.

"I'm sorry?" Morwen said.

"Tosh Hubbley," he said, this time more clearly, releasing one of the steering controls and tapping his chest. She realized it was his name.

A silence followed, as he waited for her to name herself.

"Tosca Etcheverria," she said, using another false name she had abandoned a year earlier, once she had escaped from confinement on Blatcher's World, before she became Porfiria Ardcashin, the spacer. The latter could now also be abandoned, having served its purpose.

"First time on Providence?" said Hubbley, and Morwen recognized that the price of transportation was conversation with a man who found boredom in his own company.

"Yes," she said, and hoped she could leave it at that.

"Not much to do here," he said, then left a gap for her to fill in. She made a wordless sound of affirmation and looked out the side window.

Hubbley was not deterred. "Me, I've seen a lot of it: the Bowdrey Uplands, the Tapping Plains, Coldstream Valley, the Great Gorge, the Blue Fjords. I travel, you see. My work."

He gestured with a thumb toward the vehicle's cargo compartment. Morwen looked through the rear aperture and saw boxes stacked three and four deep, each bearing a logo of a tracked vehicle and the legend: *Traffard Heavy-Duty Motilators.*

"Spare parts," Hubbley added. "They're good machines, but the filters have to be replaced regular or the fuel lines clog up."

Morwen made the same neutral sound again. Another silence ensued.

"So you're a spacer," Hubbley offered. When she didn't respond, he said, "Don't get many of them around here."

He waited again, then said, "Just visiting?"

Morwen accepted the inevitable, turned toward him. "Distant relatives. Family business."

He thought for a moment. His tone when he spoke again was cautious. "You've got people there? In New Diss?"

Morwen realized she had said more than she should have. "It's complicated."

"I imagine so," said Hubbley. "Most people with kin in New Dispensation were left behind when the Dispers relocated to Providence from Tantamount."

For a while he said nothing and just operated the vehicle. They were passing through crop lands now. Morwen saw tall spindly plants with feathery tassels at their tips and fat, fleshy leaves that began halfway up the stems. The setting sun lit the top fronds but the closely packed leaves below were dark.

Hubbley seemed to be one of the simple kind that cannot exercise the mind without the effort showing in his face. Eventually, he gave her a considering look then returned his gaze to the road ahead. "The Dispers, themselves, are not unfriendly. It's the Protectors you have to watch out for." He briefly glanced again at the cuff of her right sleeve. "You might be all right, though."

He was silent for a while, then said, "I don't know anything for sure. I go in there, deliver whatever people have ordered, and I'm on my way. I'm just saying, those Protectors, they're none too friendly toward strangers. Don't get many of them saying, 'Hey, Tosh, why don't you sit for a spell and enjoy a beverage?'"

Morwen said, "I don't intend to cause a stir."

He said, "Do you know what a weasel is?"

There was no law in the Beyond except local law, and in some places not even that. On the other side of the Pale, in the Oikumene, there was not only local and planet-wide law but an organization called the Interplanetary Police Coordinating Company. The IPCC collaborated with law enforcement bodies and provided them with research and forensic capabilities, databases that allowed criminals to be tracked from world to world, and assistance in carrying out arrests and transporting extradited felons. It also sent surreptitious agents into the Beyond to gather intelligence and even stage surgical raids to capture high-value suspects. In the Oikumene, IPCC operatives were colloquially referred to as "Ipsys." Throughout the Beyond, they were known as "weasels." Weaseling was a very dangerous occupation. Merely to be thought a weasel could be a death sentence.

"Everyone who lives in the Beyond knows what a weasel is," Morwen said.

"Then you know that strangers need to be careful. Especially in some places."

"I will be."

"Good, because New Dispensation is one of those places. Because of the business they're in."

Morwen knew that curiosity about the "business" of others was not encouraged in the Beyond. She let the conversation lapse. Sunset became dusk, became night. Hubbley turned on the forward illuminators, and the carryall rolled on. Few other vehicles passed them, none overtook them, though they were moving at a sedate velocity.

"Got to be careful driving at night," he said after a while. "Hoppers."

"Hoppers?" Morwen said.

"Local wildlife. What I've heard is they were brought here from Earth by the Originals, figured they'd eat the native plants, help clear the plains, make way for the plows."

"And?"

"Nobody knows. Maybe somebody from the Institute could study them and say for sure —" he chuckled at the absurdity "— as if you could get some Institute grandee out here. Anypart, twenty or thirty years back, something changed the beasts — something they ate, probably."

"What happened to them?"

"In a couple of generations, they stopped eating plants and started eating what ate the plants: little things that lived in burrows, and long-legged things that ran and jumped. Except the hoppers dug up all the burrows and ran down all the jumpers.

"Now they eat whatever they can catch, including each other. And including us, if we're not careful — though they tend to avoid towns, where they're shot on sight."

Morwen stared out at the tall plants. "I'd never heard about them."

"Why would you?" Hubbley said, then continued, "Sometimes they throw one of the old dams out onto the road, see if they can make you crash or turn over. Then they swarm in. Big ones can pull a door open."

Morwen said, "Perhaps you should give full attention to the road."

"I do talk too much," Hubbley said. After that, he was silent, focused on the driving.

• • •

He pointed ahead and off to the north. "Those lights behind the hills? That's New Dispensation — Mount Pleasant that was. I turn south a few minutes from here."

"Thank you for the lift," Morwen said.

"At the crossroads, that's where the hotel is — Brumble's. You'll be all right there if you lock your door."

Morwen ignored the implication. "Is there transport from the hotel to Mount... New Dispensation?"

"An omnibus comes down from Deeble whenever there are enough passengers to warrant the trip. It stops at the inn."

"Thank you again."

He was chewing over something. After a while, he said, "Watch yourself in New Diss. The local scroots are all right, but the Protectors can overrule them."

"Scroots?"

"Scrutineers. New Diss's version of a town constabulary."

Morwen nodded. "I mean to be discreet."

"You might need to be more than that. Don't ask too many questions."

He was letting the vehicle slow now. Morwen shifted in her seat, lifted her ditty bag onto her lap. "You begin to worry me."

"Good," Hubbley said. "Stay worried until you leave." He pursed his lips then added, "If they let you leave."

They arrived at the crossroads known as Brumble's Corners. Hubbley steered the car a little northward then pulled into a paved open space that surrounded a three-story building built of blond stone and black wood, the beams rough-hewn as were the blocks of masonry. Light shone from multipaned windows shielded by iron bars on the ground floor — "Hoppers," Hubbley explained. Smaller windows showed on the upper floors, few of them lit.

Several vehicles were parked in rows, most of them able to carry cargo as well as passengers, all of them showing the marks of long use.

Morwen stepped out of Tosh Hubbley's carryall, gave him another thanking and added a farewell, then climbed the flagstone steps to the inn's double doors. Inside, she found no reception desk. Instead, she entered a lamp-lit common room, with a bar to her left behind which stood a bald, round-shouldered man who interrupted his wiping of the counter to regard her with a blank expression from wet eyes.

The rest of the large room was provided with round wooden tables and chairs, most of the latter filled with men dressed in shirts, smocks, and trousers of dull-colored, sturdy cloth, an ensemble that suggested their labors never took them far from the soil. She saw cards, counters, drinking mugs, plates with the remains of suppers.

A young woman in a dirndl dress and a mobcap was clearing away the meals' detritus, loading dishes and cutlery into a square tub of dull metal on wheels. She paused and gave Morwen a quizzical glance, then frowned and looked away.

All eyes in the room, except the girl's, were turned Morwen's way, the farmers continuing to regard her with bucolic interest as she made her way to the barman.

"Are you Brumble?"

His grunt sounded like an affirmation. "Have you a room for the night?" she said.

The wet eyes turned toward the staring faces, then came back to hers. "For just yourself?" he said.

Morwen ignored the suggestion. "I presume your doors lock? And from the inside?"

The barman shrugged.

Morwen lifted her ditty bag onto the counter, loosened the cord that compressed its top, and took out a wallet. It hit the circle-stained wood with the sound of substantial coins. Then she reached in again and brought out a projac in a clip-on holster attached to a wide spacer's belt. This she buckled around her waist so that the weapon hung within easy reach.

"How much for the room and supper?" she said.

"Three svu." The currency, standard in the Oikumene as well as throughout the Beyond, was the standard value unit, each one equal to one hour's pay for an unskilled laborer. "Four, if you want glawken."

"What is glawken?"

A rattle of dishwares told Morwen that the serving woman had come near. "A hard liquor made from torquil fruit," she said. "It takes some getting used to."

Morwen saw the innkeeper frown. Some plan had just evaporated from his mind. She reached into her wallet and extracted three coins, slid them across the bar to the man's hair-bedizened hand. Then she found a fourth coin and gave it to the young woman, saying "Thank you."

The server smiled a knowing smile and tucked the money away, then rattled off along the bar toward a door.

"I'll eat in my room," Morwen said, extending a hand for the key. With her head she indicated the door through which the young woman was pushing her wheeled tub. "What's her name?"

"Madalasque," said the barman, then added, "Maddie, we calls her."

"Have Maddie bring up the food," Morwen said. She placed a hand on the butt of her projac. "Wouldn't want any misunderstandings."

Another frown from the barman, but he passed over a heavy brass key and pointed with his chin toward a door at the other end of the bar. "Stairs, two flights. Room's at the end of the corridor."

Morwen put away her wallet, closed the ditty bag, and hoisted it onto one shoulder. She turned and surveyed the room again, saw gazes drop or find other directions. Now she noticed something she had missed: at a far table, ill-lit under the mounted head of a long-necked creature with almond-shaped eyes, long ears, and protruding fangs, sat two men dressed differently from the farmers.

They wore tight-fitting shirts of some shiny material, black with blue piping, pockets, and epaulets, the collars and cuffs snug around necks and wrists. Their legs and lower torsos were clad in breeches of gray twill, buckled at the knee, below which they wore black stockings with a subdued pattern, ending in square-toed halfboots of patent leather.

The men had been watching Morwen's colloquy with the barman and looked away when she turned around. But their attitude was not like that of the rest of the assembly, who dropped their gazes diffidently. These two, narrow-headed men of a mature age, with dark hair slicked back over their ears, looked her way again and continued to study her for several heartbeats. Then they looked at each other.

Morwen climbed the stairs, found the room, and entered. She tested the lock to make sure it was sound, then inspected the place. A narrow bed covered in a well-worn quilt, a single chair but no desk, and an armoire that had once been ornate but had lost some of its wooden arabesques and inlays over a long and apparently eventful life. A faded rug covered the plank floor beside the bed, rough curtains hung over a window that gave a view of the road, the croplands, and the distant lights of what had been Mount Pleasant.

Morwen put her wallet under the flat pillow, placed her bag beside the head of the bed so she could lay the projac on its top, close to hand while she slept. Next, she sat on the bed and pulled off her boots, stretched, then interlaced her fingers on her thighs and waited.

She was practiced at waiting, and did not move until she heard a rap on the door and a female voice saying, "Sera? It's supper."

Morwen rose and opened the door, said, "Come in."

Maddie entered, carrying a tray to which were attached folding legs that created a table. She placed it in front of the single chair, then gestured to the steaming bowl of stew and the cob of bread, and said, "I put it out myself."

Morwen sat and took up a spoon. "I thank you."

The young woman shrugged, gestured toward the door and what was beyond it. "They're not really that bad," she said. "When they drink, they get ideas, but you can slap them down. In the morning, their toes turn inward and they mooch around."

The stew was hot and salty. Morwen had eaten worse. She dipped the bread in the hot liquid and bit off a soaked piece. "What about those two in the corner?"

Maddie's expression changed. "Those two," she said, with a nod and a brief look inward. "Protectors. From the new regime at New Dispensation." She corrected herself. "Well, not so new, now. The Dispers have been there seventeen, eighteen years. The Protectors, they took over the reins about ten years back."

Then she cleared her mind with a shrug and said, "They don't spend much time here. They just come when there's maunch money to collect."

"Maunch?"

"They grow it. Fact is, Dispers don't grow much else these days."

"What is it?" Morwen asked.

Now Maddie looked at Morwen as if noticing her for the first time, a long look, up and down. "You don't know what maunch is?" She studied Morwen's face, while Morwen returned her a gaze of innocence. "You're not a weasel, are you? They don't do well in New Dispensation. The Protectors." Her expression invited Morwen to reach an inevitable conclusion.

"I'm not a weasel," said Morwen. "Just a spacer, passing through."

"Protectors will kill you, if you are," Maddie said. "Even if you aren't, they might kill you in their efforts to find out."

There was only one interworld organization in the Beyond: the Deweaseling Corps, numbering hundreds of highly intelligent and completely vicious operatives, was expert in the skills of interrogation and torture. Its personnel could be summoned to any world where the IPCC was suspected of having infiltrated its agents, or they might arrive on their own initiative. The Corps also regularly trained local authorities in its techniques, providing refresher courses. In places where those local authorities oversaw criminal activities, the application of deweaseling practices created unfortunate results for persons who wandered into those territories.

Better safe than sorry was the Deweaseling Corps's motto. The safety did not extend to suspected weasels.

Morwen repeated, "I'm just a spacer, but I come from deep in the Beyond, and have only been a year off. . . my home world." Now it was her turn to study her interlocutor, to see if her brief hesitation had triggered any reaction. It appeared it hadn't.

Morwen continued, "Providence is the closest I've been to the Pale and the Oikumene. There's a lot I don't know."

Maddie's mouth turned sideways a little as she took this in, then her shoulders moved in a gesture of acceptance.

"Maunch is what brought the Dispers to Providence," she said, "that and the fact that there was an entire town standing empty. Nobody had ever gone there, once they'd buried the bodies. It would have been like walking on a grave."

"I know about the raid," Morwen said, keeping her voice neutral. "Everybody knows about the Demon Princes and Mount Pleasant."

Everybody, Maddie said, included the adherents of the Doctrine of the New Dispensation. These were a tight-knit society that had arisen on one of the worlds of the Rigel Concourse — either Tantamount or Xion, she wasn't sure — but their ethos had clashed with those of neighboring communities.

The cause of the disagreements was maunch. Formerly, it was a herb that grew wild in the tropics of the Dispers' world of origin, and was picked by locals who chewed it for its mild psychedelic qualities. Then a visitor from another region encountered the drug's effect and carried back some samples, roots and all, to his home.

His name was Porleth Armbruch and his home happened to include a well furnished laboratory, the fellow being an instructor in natural chemistry at a collegium. He grew new plants from his specimens and began to experiment with altering maunch's gene plasm. The result: with the addition of a few extra molecules, he created a much more potent version of the mind-expander.

When Armbruch tried the new substance, Maddie related, he was cast out of the universe into a new realm. A disembodied voice addressed him by name, telling him that he had been chosen to deliver unto humanity a new dispensation that would free them from all misery.

"I know this," Maddie said, "because the Dispers used to come to our meeting house every Contemplation Day and harangue the parishioners. Finally, they were met by a crowd armed with tools and told to take their New Dispensation home and keep it there.

"There was ill feeling for a while, but the Dispers came to understand that it would serve them not at all to be driven from another world so soon after they arrived. So we agreed to live and let live, and now we get along. Some of us even go to their Fifthday dances. When it was Mount Pleasant, the original farmers used to ship their produce by barge along the Parmell River. Now our farmers truck the Dispers' maunch to New Hambledon along with our leeks and sweetpods, our chupi melons and sassafranch. We sell it to offworlders for a good price and keep twenty percent."

The "offworlders," it appeared, were criminals who sold maunch on several worlds of the Oikumene where there was both a lucrative market and a prohibition on its importation. They had warned the Dispers that agents of the Interplanetary Police Coordinating Company — known as weasels throughout the Beyond — would try to disrupt the illicit trade.

Morwen, having grown up on Blatcher's World, a haven for pirates and slavers, knew what everyone in the Beyond knew: the Deweaseling Corps was generally skilled at identifying and neutralizing the agents the IPCC sent from the Oikumene. And what the Deweaseling Corps lacked in skill it made up for in viciousness. Identification was always followed by harsh interrogation to acquire new intelligence as to the IPCC's operations. The interrogations were often followed by summary execution. Morwen had seen two such killings in the town square of Boregore, near to the estate where she had grown up.

Maddie was well informed. As the maunch-peddling enterprise grew in the scope of its interworld outreach, she said, the Corps sent experienced deweaselers to instruct some of the Dispers in the techniques of deweaseling. These trainees were mostly Protectors, identifiable by their black and blue uniforms and uncompromising attitudes, but the town constabulary of New Diss, the scrutineers (or scroots), had also been trained.

"The Protectors see any newcomers as suspect," Maddie said. "They're liable to take immediate action, if you know what I mean. You should stay away from New Diss." She looked at the door. "You might not be safe there — or here, now that those two downstairs saw you."

"I'm not a weasel," Morwen reminded her.

"That probably wouldn't matter," Maddie said. "Better safe than sorry, they say." She cocked her head and said, "Brumble's calling me." She crossed to the door, opened it, and said, "Leave the tray outside the room." She began to leave, stopped, turned, and added, "If anyone knocks, better not answer the door."

Morwen lifted the projac from beside her bed. The motion again caused her sleeve to ride up and she saw Maddie's eyes drawn to her tattoo. But the young woman suppressed any reaction and left. Morwen rose and locked the door.

In the morning, Morwen went to the ablutory at the end of the hall, relieved herself and cleaned up, her projac never far out of reach. When she returned to her room she found Maddie waiting outside, a bundle under her arm.

"If you go to New Dispensation wearing spacer gear," she said, "you'll stand out like a pimple on a flibbet's nose."

"Flibbet?"

"What I used to be before I left school and became this." Maddie gestured with her free hand to the faded dirndl dress.

"I'm not sure that would be any better than what I have on," Morwen said.

That brought a "Huh!" and a chuckle. Maddie pinched some of the dress's fabric. "This is only to work in. I was a farm girl and looked it."

Morwen unlocked the door and they went in. Maddie's bundle turned out to include a knee-length skirt of heavy homespun, a pale-yellow cotton blouse printed with red and blue blossoms, and a sleeveless vest, green with yellow edging, that closed with loops of twisted cord. Knee-length stockings that matched the vest and a hat of stiff linen, complexly folded, completed the ensemble.

"Your boots are close enough to local wear. Just don't draw attention to them."

"No kicks or saltations," Morwen said, with a wry smile. "Understood."

"Take it seriously," Maddie said.

Morwen reached out, touched the young woman's arm. "I do. And I thank you for considering my well-being." She found her wallet and extracted a five-svu certificate.

Maddie waved it away. "They're only a loan. You can give them back before you leave."

"What if the deweaselers take me up? You might not want them then."

Maddie sighed and took the certificate, tucked it into her bodice. "Don't let that happen," she said. "I really like to wear that vest when I go out dancing."

Breakfast was porridge and bacon, washed down with sour ale or a green tea that tasted tart and peppery. Morwen was enjoying her second cup when the omnibus rolled in from the north and pulled up outside the inn. She hoisted her ditty bag and looked about for Maddie, meaning to say goodbye, but a clatter of dishware from behind the kitchen door said the server was occupied.

Wearing her borrowed clothes, Morwen stepped out into the gray morning, the sun barely risen above the chain of hills that included the broad elevation that had given Mount Pleasant its original name. The omnibus was a long vehicle, yellow with red stripes, mounted on eight inflatable wheels as tall as Morwen. She climbed a set of steps that led to where the driver sat, paid him the fare he asked for, and took a seat at the rear of the compartment.

The projac tucked into the waistband of Maddie's skirt galled her back, so she took it out, put it on her lap, and rested the ditty bag on it. None of the other passengers, all with the look of country folk except for one man who sat halfway up the aisle, paid her any out-of-the-ordinary attention. She studied the back of his corded neck for a while and ultimately decided he had no interest in her. She returned the weapon to the bag.

They waited a little while, but no one else boarded at the inn. The driver sounded his klaxon twice, waited another brief interval, then put the vehicle into gear and steered it out onto the road.

The omnibus rolled quietly, except for the swish of its great tires on the pavement. Morwen gazed out the window at the fields under the brightening day. She felt a growing sense of dissociation: she was entering a landscape she knew, though she had never been here. Images that had been inculcated in her mind during her childhood were now encountering the reality on which they had been based.

Here was the crossroads marked by a spreading horcanthria tree, with a bole-ringing wooden bench for foot-travelers to rest on in the heat of the day, and next to it the simple hand pump that would draw refreshing cold water from underground. It was much as she had imagined it. Not mentioned in her education was a stout cudgel hung on a cord suspended from a nail driven into the trunk, its business end stained red. *Hoppers*, Morwen assumed.

Not far beyond the horcanthria, the road began to rise toward the hills, dominated by the great broad hump of Mount Pleasant. Morwen's father had drawn it for her, along with many other sites he recreated from memory. It, too, was recognizable, for all the difference between the sketch and the reality.

Now the road leveled off for a stretch, crossing a saddle between two hills. Off to the right, down a dirt lane, was Rolf Gersen's farm, with its great barn, looking much as it had been described to her. There was a difference, though: a broad stretch of land running down to the river had been pasture for the Gersens' dairy herd; now it held row upon row of greenhouses, their panes glinting in the sun.

More fields now, separated from the road and from each other by head-high stone walls. Srivana's Wood on the left, maples, sweet chestnuts, and smoothreds, looking neglected, untended for many years. Then the road descended into the Hollow, with a high and wide wooden bridge crossing the placid Parmell River, derelict barges hauled up on shore or left to sink where they'd been moored the day the space pirates came.

And now the road rose to enter the town itself, in a natural amphitheater ringed by seven hills, including the broad almost-mountain for which the place had been named. Morwen looked at the familiar sights she was seeing for the first time, and remembered her father saying that it had never occurred to the inhabitants of Mount Pleasant that their geography created a ready-made corral, ideal for men with projacs, neuronic whips, and tumblethrusts to land their ships on the edges of town and herd everyone into the center — then call down the carriers and take them away to be sold in the slave markets of Barrantroy, New Fogo, and Interchange.

The main street of Mount Pleasant, Broadway, was as it had been described to Morwen, except that many of the shops stood empty. But the town's only restaurant was open for business, though the sign above the windows said it was now known as The Eatery. And the community hall had been recently repainted. A sign outside the wire-fenced playground in the hall's forecourt said, *Social Dance, Fifthday, 7 pm* and *Meet-Up Firstday 10 am, Sacrament 9 am.*

The omnibus slowed, then with a hiss of brakes it stopped at an intersection outside what Morwen recognized as the town hall, built of red brick with a steel roof painted green. A flight of steps led up to the double doors of black ganfo, the wood scarred by the signatures of energy weapons. The hall had also housed the Mount Pleasant jail and constabulary, all of whose members had died in a vain attempt to defend their fellow townsfolk.

Across from the hall was the hotel. Morwen was surprised to see that its sign still read *The Llanko Inn*, as it had been named when her parents stayed there immediately after their arrival. The omnibus's front door stood open and Morwen was the only passenger to descend from the vehicle. She entered the hotel straight away. The reception area was small, shabby but clean, and she was sure that every appurtenance she was seeing had been here since the raid. A gray-haired woman stood behind the desk, a stylus raised over the registry book as if she had been in the midst of some writing when the unexpected suddenly hove into view. A sign in front of the registry read, *Dedana Llanko*.

The suddenly unexpected must be Morwen, because the woman's raised brows now descended into a compressed chevron as the new arrival crossed the worn carpet, stood her ditty bag against the veneer panel that fronted the reception desk, and said, "I'd like a room with its own facilities, please."

At first she thought the woman was going to turn her away, then she saw a change of strategy. "How long for?" was the response.

"My plans are not yet formed," Morwen said. "At least a few days, maybe more."

She was being sharply scrutinized now. "Depending on what?"

"Does that matter?"

"The scroots will ask me," said the woman. "Probably the Protectors, too. What will I tell them?"

"You can tell them," Morwen said, with a pause for emphasis, "to ask me."

That brought a grunt. The woman reached down below the counter between them and brought up a card of stiff paper. "Name?" she said.

Morwen became Porfiria Ardcashin once more, giving her address as a house she had once stayed at for a week in Biddles Town on Vladimir, while the *Festerlein* was having its holds fumigated and its galley rid of an infestation of arthropods that came aboard with a cargo of teetee pods. She watched as the information was carefully recorded.

"I'll pay a week in advance," she said.

"You certainly will," said the old woman, setting down the stylus and slipping the card into one of several slots that made up a wood frame attached to the wall beside her. From the same slot, she fetched a key and stood holding it in expectation. "Twenty-one SVU."

Morwen brought out her wallet and counted out certificates and one coin. The key was handed over and she was directed to climb the stairs and take the first door on the right. The woman went back to the papers in front of her, as if the guest had ceased to exist.

Morwen climbed the stairs, its carpet held in place by brass rods and smelling of disinfectant and old wool. The door to her room was loose in its frame, as if it had dried out over the years. The lock was sturdy enough, but probably easy to pick.

She opened a free-standing wardrobe that took up most of one wall and was rewarded with a waft of the sharp scent of furniture polish. The narrow bed was hard but there was an overstuffed armchair to rest in. She hung up her spacer's garb and put away her small clothes in the drawers at the bottom of the armoire. She decided to keep the projac handy.

The window looked out on a street that crossed Broadway and ran past the old town hall: Mallaby Lane, she remembered as its name. Mallaby ran on, straight toward the low hills to the south, passing between two of them, until it met the ring road that circumscribed Mount Pleasant. Beyond that lay fields and woodlots, but again Morwen saw greenhouses where she had been told to expect open land.

She laid her head against the side of the window so she could peer north along Mallaby. The glass distorted her view, but she could just make out where the straight street left town and became a series of switchbacks climbing the eminence for which the town had once been named. Halfway up was a blob of white.

"And there it is," she said to herself.

The door rattled as someone on the other side struck it three hard blows — a fist, not knuckles.

Morwen tucked the projac under the pillow on the bed. "And here we go," she said. She opened the door but stood, leaning against the jamb, in a silent denial of entry.

She was expecting Protectors, clad in black and blue. Instead, she saw two men in dark shirts and gray breeches. Around their waists were buckled wide black belts from which hung the paraphernalia common to police agents in both the Oikumene and the Beyond.

One of them, a little older than the other and with an intelligent face assembled from hard planes, held the card the old woman had filled in at the reception desk. He glanced at it now and said, "Porfiria Ardcashin?" as if it were a comic collation of syllables.

"That's right," Morwen said.

"From…" He read from the card, "Biddles Town on Vladimir?"

"Uh-huh. Who are you?"

"Leading Scrutineer Eldo Kronik." He looked at her the way police look at those they suspect of malfeasance — which, in the Beyond, could be anyone and was often a safe bet. Morwen saw him decide to leap past the preliminaries.

"What are you doing in New Dispensation?"

Morwen let her face show mild puzzlement. "What does one do in a town like this?" she said. "I intend to see the sights, absorb the ambience, profit from new experiences."

The scrutineer stepped closer, until his face was less than a hand's width from Morwen's. "If that was meant to be amusing, it failed. I will now ask you one more time: what are you doing here?"

He stepped back and put a hand on a holstered weapon.

Morwen had an explanation ready. She had signed on as an ordinary spacer on a tramp freighter. She named it. Because she could cook — "My parents once ran a restaurant," — she had been assigned to be assistant to the ship's cook.

"All was well for the first few voyages. But the captain, who was also the owner, eventually revealed himself as a 'man with a horn,' if you know what I mean. I got tired of being chased around the galley. I resolved that come the next world we put into, I would jump ship, find a place to lie low until the *Festerlein* departed, then return to the spaceport and find a new berth."

"You're a cook?"

"So I said, though on the ship I was cook's flunky."

The scrutineer looked at the card again, then back to Morwen. "Come with us."

"Am I being arrested? I have done nothing wrong."

"Not arrested," said the man, with a smile. "Tested. We're going to the restaurant across the street."

• • •

Breakfast was finished and it was still too early for lunch. A wiry, dark-haired man in a calf-length apron and cloth hat, both once white but now stained beyond redemption, was sweeping the floor while a red-haired woman in a cotton-print dress and apron was wiping down a table. They looked up in slight surprise as the two scrutineers escorted Morwen through the door.

"Kronik?" said the man. "We're not serving yet."

"We're not here to eat," said the older man. He pushed Morwen down past the counter with its row of stools and through the swinging door to the kitchen, beckoning to the man in the apron to follow.

The kitchen was adequately equipped, the cleanser humming as it washed the breakfast dishes. The counters were clean, with nothing on them except the remains of some animal's leg, that Morwen assumed was last night's roast.

Scrutineer Kronik said to the man in the apron, "Gisby, I want you to choose some stuff at random, greens, roots, whatever."

Gisby's face registered puzzlement. "Why?"

"Never mind why. Just do it."

The cook went to a walk-in larder, stepped in, and emerged with handfuls of green stuff.

"Lay them on the counter."

Morwen saw some sad-looking leeks, some greens that resembled parsley, a few small potatoes. Gisby stepped back, his expression showing that he was waiting for an explanation.

Kronik said to Morwen, "All right, you're a cook, cook that."

"What?" she said.

"Make something out of that. A good cook can make something out of anything."

Morwen studied the ingredients, lifted the sort-of-parsley and sniffed. It smelled a little like thyme. She turned to Gisby. "Is that meat like lamb?"

"A little gamier," was the answer. "It's called shumkin."

Morwen remembered the name. It was a species of herbivore native to Providence that the early settlers had domesticated.

She thought for a minute, then said, "I could make a stew. Got any garlic?"

Gisby gestured to a wall-mounted rack that held small bottles. "Powdered," he said. "Doesn't grow well, but we import it from off-world."

"No problem," Morwen said. "Give me a knife."

Kronik stepped back, his hand going to his holstered weapon, unhooking the flap.

Morwen paid him no heed. She took the leeks and chopped them into fine pieces, the blade going up and down at high speed and with precision. Then she did the same to the herb. She sliced meat from the bone and cut it into cubes, then cut the potatoes into bite-sized chunks.

She reached for a steel bowl, combined all the ingredients, and flavored the mix with garlic and ground pepper from the spices rack. She sniffed the result and grunted softly.

Then she turned to Gisby and said, "I'm thinking this will make a decent stew, but it would make a better pie. Have you got some pastry?"

Gisby took the bowl from her, sniffed for himself, and said, "In the cooler."

He opened an enameled door and brought out some rolls of ready-made pastry, sprinkled some flour from a container on a wooden cutting board, and handed the pastry to Morwen. "Rolling pin's in that drawer."

"Put the oven on," she said.

Not long after, Morwen put a filled pie, its top fluted along the edges, into the oven. To Gisby, she said, "You know your oven. What do you think?"

"Forty minutes?"

She turned to Kronik, saw a scowl. "So, am I a cook?" she said.

Gisby answered before the scrutineer could, "She's a cook."

Kronik grunted a reluctant acceptance. "We're not finished. No reason a weasel can't cook."

Gisby said, "Well, when you're finished, you can send her back here." To Morwen, he said, "You've got a job here any time you want it."

"Maybe so," she said. She looked to the scrutineer. "Let's go finish," she said.

Chapter Two

The back reaches of the town hall housed the constabulary. Kronik went first down the corridor, with his deputy bringing up the rear. As they passed a squad room, he beckoned to a female constable and said, "Toba, in my office."

Morwen proceeded docilely and was led into a small room with a plain table and four chairs.

"Hands against the wall," the scrutineer said, followed by a quick frisking by the female constable that was not as invasive as it might have been. At Kronik's gesture, she sat. Kronik sat across from her while his subordinate stayed behind, out of her line of sight.

"When you were cutting up the vegetables," Kronik said, "I noticed a mark on your wrist. Pull up your sleeve."

The moment had been bound to arrive. Morwen did as she was bidden, and Kronik beckoned for her to extend her arm. He studied the tattoo, then read what was written on her flesh, " 'Property of Hacheem Belloch, Boregore, Blatcher's World. Reward for recovery.' I take it the circular design is his sigil."

"It is," Morwen said.

"I'm not familiar with Blatcher's World."

She pulled down her sleeve, covering the tattoo. "It's deep in the Beyond. Belloch controls a large part of it and influences the parts he doesn't control."

"And I take it you were not emancipated by Ser Belloch."

"No. I escaped."

Kronik regarded her for a moment. She could see he was adding the information to his assessment of her. "How did you come to be enslaved?"

"I was born into it."

"Your parents belonged to Hacheem Belloch?"

Morwen nodded.

"And were they born to it, too?"

She shook her head. "They were stolen in a pirate raid."

Kronik leaned back in his chair. A silence grew while the scrutineer studied her. Then he said, "There was a pirate raid here, when this place was called Mount Pleasant."

Morwen met his gaze. "I know."

"Do I make the right assumption?"

Her eyes still on his, she nodded again.

His forefinger tapped thoughtfully on the tabletop. "All properties in this municipality were declared abandoned and *terra nulla* by the regional governate ten years after the raid," he said.

Morwen shrugged. "My parents arrived a few months before the raid. They were tenants. They owned no land. There is no property for me to reclaim."

"The Corporation of the New Dispensation holds legal title to the entire town and the surrounding farms," Kronik said.

"I'm not here to make any claims," she said.

"Then why are you here?"

She pulled up her sleeve and showed the words written there. "Where else am I to go?" she said.

Kronik gave the bridge of his nose a thoughtful stroke. "So the tale about the 'man with a horn' was false?"

"Not that part," Morwen said. "I would have jumped ship anyway, but a chance to see where my parents came from…" She spread her hands.

"Huh," said the scrutineer.

When Morwen reentered the restaurant, the aroma of seasoned meat filled the air. Gisby and his wife sat at a back table, Morwen's pie between them. They were forking up bites of pastry and its filling. "This is good," said the cook.

"Really good," said his wife, around a mouthful. She chewed and swallowed, then said, "I'm Terelia."

"Morwen Sabine." There was no point keeping Porfiria in play after naming herself to the scrutineers.

"Do you want the job?" Gisby said.

"I think so. I'll be staying for a while and need to do something."

Terelia pushed a chair toward Morwen with one foot. "Sit down. Have some pie." She took another fork from a nearby place setting and handed it to Morwen.

"Besides," said Gisby, "there's nothing much to do except grow maunch, and they're not going to let a newcomer do that."

"That's a certainty," said his wife. "It's not like it used to be."

Morwen took a bite of her pie. It *was* good. The flavors had melded as she had known they would.

"Old family recipe?" Terelia said.

"No. I'd never heard of... what's the meat called?"

"Shumkin."

"Never heard of shumkin before. Or the herb."

"Pickmegreen," Gisby said.

"But I knew they'd go together well. I have a flair for flavors, my dad used to say."

"Was he a cook?" Terelia said.

Morwen nodded, mouth full of a second bite of pie.

"Where?" Gisby said.

Chewing, Morwen moved a forefinger in a circle, as if drawing a small ring on the ceiling tiles. Then she swallowed and said, "Here."

Gis by and Terelia looked at each other then back to Morwen. "Right here?" Terelia asked.

"This was theirs," Morwen said.

Gisby spoke without combativeness. "It's legally ours."

"I know. I'm not here to take it back."

Terelia's expression had hardened to wariness. "Then why are you here?"

Morwen sighed. "Because it is a lot better than where I was." She pulled up her sleeve and showed them the ownership mark of Hacheem Belloch. "He owns my parents. I mean to make enough to buy them — and myself — out of bondage."

Again, Gisby and Terelia exchanged a look. The man cleared his throat to say something, but at that point the bell over the door jangled as three men in work clothing entered and called greetings to the proprietors. They moved to a table by the window, pulled out chairs, and seated themselves with an air of familiarity.

Two of them reached for the menu cards stood upright in the wire frame that contained bottles and shakers of condiments. The third said, "What's the special?"

Gisby said to Morwen. "There's more leftover shumkin. Do you want to make another pie? Or maybe three of them?"

"All right," she said.

The three rose from the table. Terelia went behind the counter, to where a carafe of the hot and mildly addictive drink called punge, drunk all over the Oikumene and the Beyond, stood on a warmer. She brought it to the customers' table and poured without asking.

"You can have something quick-fried," she told them, "but if you're willing to wait, the special's going to be a treat."

As the day wore on into evening, the Eatery grew busy. Morwen's pies were a success, as was a sweet and spicy salad dressing she whipped up from a light oil, honey, and a couple of choices from the spice rack. Gisby and Terelia went back and forth, serving, the man taking time to shake the basket of deep-fried freshwater whelks from the Parmell River and to prepare thin galettes of black wheat to wrap them in.

Morwen worked as hard as she ever had in the freighter's galley or the kitchens of Hacheem Belloch. By the time the last dishes were in the washer and the counters all wiped down, she was ready for bed.

As Morwen headed for the door, waving a good night, Terelia said, "There's a suite upstairs. We used to live here before we bought our house on Tybald Street. It's a little dusty but it's all set up. You're welcome to it. Free."

As she spoke, she reached for a set of keys hanging on the wall beside the clock. When Morwen stopped, she tossed her the keys. "The door's around the corner."

Morwen caught the keys, thanked her, and went across the street to reclaim her ditty bag. Sera Llanko gave her a sour look when she said she was checking out and asked for her deposit back, but she counted out the money, "Less six svu for wear and tear."

Morwen was too tired to argue. She climbed the stairs, unlocked her door, and found Kronik seated in the armchair, her projac in his lap.

"You didn't mention this," he said.

"You didn't ask."

"No weapons are allowed in the town limits."

Morwen shrugged. "Then take it. I don't expect I'll need to shoot anyone."

"Come by the constabulary tomorrow," Kronik said. "I'll give you a receipt."

During the interrogation earlier, she had told the scrutineers of how she had escaped from Blatcher's World by stowing away on a tramp freighter when it took on a cargo of rare hardwoods and crates of a fine-grained clay, unique to that planet, that was prized by potters on a dozen worlds. Captain Izzich would have returned her to captivity and claimed the reward, except when she demonstrated that she could cook, he signed her on at half-pay and reduced the man who had been desecrating the freighter's galley to ordinary cargo roustabout.

The deposed cook had promised revenge, but the rest of the crew had been won over by Morwen's cuisine and had let him know that if anything happened to her, he would soon after "cold walk" — spacers' slang for being put out of an airlock without a suit.

Later, after she had acquired false papers, she signed on with the *Festerlein*, another tramp that went wherever there was a cargo to be had.

Now Kronik said, "It is a good story, and we will check it as best we can. In the meantime, you can have the freedom of the town, as I said earlier. You will not leave without authorization. And you will not go near the maunch, nor will you pry into the mechanics of that trade."

"I told you, I'm not a weasel. I don't care about your maunch smuggling."

The scrutineer smiled a cynical smile. "Exactly what a weasel would say. I also advise you to avoid the Manse."

"I don't know what that is."

Kronik gestured toward the window. "That big pile of stone up the hill. It's where Jerz Thanda and his Protectors play their games." The thought brought a deeper frown to his face.

In her parents' time, the Manse had been a semi-luxurious hotel. "All I want is to earn enough to go to Interchange and buy my parents out of Belloch's grasp."

"But that would be a lot of svu. Not likely to earn that as a cook in a small town cafe."

"I'll find a way," Morwen said. "I've come this far against the odds."

Kronik nodded, not in agreement with her but in accord with whatever thoughts were occupying his mind. He rose and went to the door, stopped and turned back.

"One thing," he said. "We have no arrangements with whoever runs things on Blatcher's World. But if Belloch finds out you are here, he may send someone to bring you back."

"I know," said Morwen. "He believes in holding what is his." She raised a hand and clenched it into a fist, so that her knuckles turned white.

"We may have to decide whether or not to let that happen."

"Then I had better not be a trouble to you."

Kronik opened the door. "My thought exactly. Good cooks are hard to find."

Life at the Eatery settled into the routine that human metabolism combined with cultural norms usually established, throughout the Beyond as well as in the Oikumene. The place served three sittings a day: breakfast, lunch, and dinner. For each, the tables and counter spaces were usually filled, a sign there was plenty of money in New Dispensation. Before each sitting, there was prep to do; after each, there was clean-up.

In between, there were periods when the door was closed and Gisby, Terelia, and Morwen were at leisure. Morwen spent hers walking about the town, as a new inhabitant should, getting to know the place and its inhabitants, purchasing local clothes and a second set of footwear. The physical layout of New Dispensation she already knew, that knowledge having been drilled into her since toddlerhood. The people she was getting to know, and finding them not as strange as she had anticipated when Maddie had told her about the cult of the New Dispensation.

The religion — or philosophy, she was not yet sure which — sat lightly upon the Dispers. They did not have to wear distinctive garb or perform rituals several times a day. Their speech was like anyone's, down to the curses and idioms that pervaded human space. They maintained a temple that they called the meet-up, in a building that in Morwen's parents' time had been a community hall, but did not seem to have a permanent clergy. There was not even an emblem or a sign to denote the structure's function, other than the schedule out front.

On Firstday, no work was done in the morning after breakfast. The Dispers gathered in the high-raftered hall and sat on rows of benches or stood around the walls. Up on the small stage at the front of the big room, a few members of the community perched on wooden chairs. Before the gathering, they had ingested the sacramental maunch and, as it activated their neural pathways toward unusual destinations, they revealed to the congregation whatever insights occurred to them.

To Morwen, invited but not pressured to intend, the revelations ranged from the mundane to the absurd, but the Dispers accepted them with nods and hums of interest, and sometimes mild-voiced affirmations. After an hour or two, the substance began to lose its grip on the celebrants' minds, and they rose from the chairs and departed. So did the rest of the assembly, amid a buzz of low-voiced commentary, punctuated by chuckles and occasional outbursts of laughter.

Then everyone returned to their normal routines. Back at the restaurant, clearing away the remains of breakfast, Terelia asked Morwen what she thought of her first brush with the New Dispensation.

She answered honestly, "I'm not sure what to think. It was like watching the surface of a pond, seeing a few flitters darting about and sometimes a bubble breaking through from the depths, but not knowing what lies below."

"Fair comment," said Terelia. "We've all chewed the sacrament, so we know what ways it opens. We understand where the explorers are going, because we've all been there."

She looked thoughtful for a moment. "Actually, it's different now. When we were on Tantamount, being persecuted for our beliefs, the sights were more stark. Now that we've been here for a few years, there's a kind of mellowness to the sightseeing. Wouldn't you say, Gis?"

Gisby allowed as how that might be so. "Even Eldo Kronik is not so tightly wound as he used to be."

"He's gotten over…you know who," Terelia said.

Morwen gathered that "explorers" referred to the people on the stage. They were not chosen. They were fellow congregants who felt the need — or perhaps just the urge — to chew the drug and report on the visions or epiphanies it conjured up in them. Every adult member of the community had played that role, and some of them were renowned for the power of the experiences they related.

"Wait until you hear Palu Gurber," Gisby said. "He goes places… Well, you'd need to have sightseen to understand it."

"Sightseen?" Morwen said. "Does that mean having 'chewed the maunch'?"

"Yes. 'Seeing the sights' is how the Initiator first put it. That was Porleth Armbruch, the prophet who led us here."

At the mention of the name, both Gisby's and Terelia's faces took on a cast Morwen had seen on those who remembered fondly someone who had "gone on," as the expression was on Blatcher's World.

"He's no longer with you?" she said.

"Alas, no," said Terelia. "An accident with his car. It was a sad day for the congregation. We lost our great guide." Morwen saw her put the matter behind her. "Jerz Thanda took over the leadership. It was what Porleth wanted, he told us. But…"

Gisby waved a hand in a way that said his wife's "but" should not be elaborated on. Terelia took a breath and said, "Well, that's enough lipflap. Let's get this place in good order."

She stacked some smeared dishes and carried them off to the kitchen. Gisby watched her go, then beckoned Morwen to follow him to the counter. He poured a mug of punge then picked up a spoon and began to stir the liquid, even though he had not put any sweetness into it. The spoon made a loud clinking against the crockery.

He spoke, softly, "You'll know more when you've been here longer, but loose talk about Porleth's accident or Jerz Thanda…"

His head turned as if to spot someone who might be listening, though he and Morwen were alone at the counter. He made a gesture that combined dismissal with a vague warning. "Enough said, understood?"

"As you say," Morwen said, and began to wipe down the counter.

• • •

When she was not working or getting to know the town, Morwen spent her time in the little apartment above the restaurant. It contained a sitting room, a bedroom, a small kitchen, and a rudimentary ablutory. The sitting room and bedroom each had a window that faced north. In the former, she would position herself on a chair and study the view that she had memorized since childhood.

The wooden house, painted white long ago but now faded, appeared to be abandoned. Before the raid by the Demon Princes and their henchmen, Mount Pleasant had a population of some five thousand, virtually all of whom had been taken to the slave markets deep in the Beyond. The Dispers numbered no more than two thousand, and had tended to settle in the built-up part of the townsite. Many of the outlying farm houses had been left empty, although the pastures and croplands were put to use as the sites of the ubiquitous greenhouses in which they grew the maunch for Jerz Thanda.

Morwen's parents had lived in the white house. Morwen knew its interior layout and the grounds that surrounded it to the last detail. One of those details was the lightning-blasted oak that stood beside the long, unpaved lane that led to the property's front gate. Her parents had been concerned that someone might have cut down the tortured tree and used it for firewood.

But that had not happened, and so Morwen's and her parents' plan had passed one crucial test. The second would come soon, she hoped, once she was accepted as a normal feature of the landscape whose movements would not draw suspicion. She would need a pair of heavy gloves, however.

They were setting up for lunch on Fourthday. Breakfast had been busy. The fritters Morwen had introduced as a side dish had been well received, as had her new entree: bacon-and-egg pie. She was in the kitchen, peeling and chopping kirstroot for the lunch special and half-listening to Gisby and Terelia chattering about nothing very much, amid a succession of musical clinks that said they were setting the tables with glassware and cutlery.

Morwen heard the jangle of the bell above the door and expected to hear, "We're closed," from one or both of the owners. Instead she heard silence, and instantly it threw her back into those times when one of Belloch's slaves had done something that caught the attention of Vilch, the head overseer. A dropped plate, a spill of wine, even a sneeze at the wrong moment. Then everyone would freeze and fall silent, waiting for the quietly voiced question, the trembling answer, and then the sudden plummet into cold-hearted violence. Or worse, an appointment with the whip.

This was one of those silences. Knife in hand, Morwen went to the kitchen door and opened it. Terelia and Gisby were standing motionless, their hands full of tableware. Just closing the door behind him was a man dressed in a Protectors' black tunic with blue piping and buttons of polished jet all down its front, over blue breeches, black stockings, and calf-high boots.

He turned toward Morwen as she appeared in the kitchen doorway and she felt the impact of his gaze as almost a physical shock. His face was pale, skin stretched tight over bone, the nose a hooked blade, and the eyes under heavy brows were as hard and bright as the buttons on his chest.

His voice was dry, almost a whisper, but it carried well in the silence: "I am Thanda. You're the newcomer."

"I am," she said. "Morwen Sabine."

"An abscondee, so I hear."

"By the law on Blatcher's World, if I manage to remain free for a standard year, I am legally self-emancipated."

A mere hint of a smile twitched the thin-lipped mouth, then disappeared. "An interesting concept. Does it happen often?"

"No."

"Come here and show me your arm."

Morwen put down the knife and came around the counter, tugged up her sleeve and presented the tattoo. Thanda took hold of her arm and rubbed a cold thumb over the markings.

She said, "It's real. The dye goes all the way down to the fascia. Remove the skin, apply a graft, and the tattoo will gradually reappear. Hacheem Belloch takes no half-measures."

He let her arm drop and motioned for her to back away. He studied her from toe to head. "What are you doing here?" He emphasized the last word.

"It was chance. The freighter I was on went wherever it had a cargo to deliver. When I heard that we were going to put in at Providence, it seemed, well, like..."

"Fate?" said the man in black. "Destiny?"

Morwen shrugged. "Something like that."

"And now here you are," he said. "And they tell me your family lived here, before the immolation."

"The what?"

His pale hand made an indolent gesture. "The mass abduction."

"My parents lived here." She made a gesture of her own. "This was their business."

"A remarkable coincidence."

"Yes, I suppose it is. They are known to occur."

His face now became that of a man who grappled with a troubling abstract theorem. "And can you prove any of it?"

"I have no documents," Morwen said, "other than my spacer's card, and that is in a false name."

"Indeed? A false name?"

"If I'd registered under my real name, Hacheem Belloch's agents would soon have found me and returned me to servitude. Or done worse, to discourage others from running."

"So 'Porfiria Ardcashin' was a made-up name."

"It was."

"Whereas Morwen Sabine is not?"

"It is who I am."

Thanda raised a finger as if to herald an important point. "And it happens to match that of the man in whose name this establishment was licensed, before the raid."

Morwen folded her arms across her chest. "It does not 'happen' so. It *is* so. He is my father."

"Is? He still lives?"

"I have told all this to Leading Scrutineer Kronik."

"And now you will tell it to me."

So, she did. Her plan to flee servitude, make her way to the Oikumene, earn enough to go to Interchange and buy her family and herself out of captivity.

When she had finished, Thanda said, "A tale fit for the fiction of derring-do."

Morwen made no reply, but kept her gaze locked onto his. After a moment, he said, "But how is *this* part of the plan, earning a cook's wages on a world far from the Oikumene?"

"As I said, when I learned we were stopping on Providence, something impelled me to come to where my parents lived."

"As you said: fate, destiny, wyrd." He stroked his chin. "Possible," he said. "You have been walking about, touching walls, viewing vistas, sitting on benches."

Morwen took in a breath, sighed. "I think to myself: was it here my parents walked, here they sat and held hands, here they discovered I was in my mother's womb?"

Thanda formed his lips into a skeptical moue. "First fate, now romanticism."

Morwen said nothing, affecting a neutral gaze as slaves will do before a power that may strike them with impunity.

Thanda opened a new line of inquiry. "Where did your parents live?"

"If you've consulted the records, you already know."

"I do know. Now I want to know if you do."

Morwen gestured with her head. "The white house, with the blasted tree."

Thanda's nod confirmed it. "It stands empty, yet you haven't visited there."

"Kronik told me to remain within the town limits."

Thanda showed the face of a man who plays a complex game in which the opponent has made an expected move. "You obey the scrutineer, but you fled your owner. You obey some authorities, not others."

"Belloch's 'ownership' was illicit. Not an authority, just a power."

"Ah, a sophist," said Thanda. "We should get together and plumb the philosophical depths."

Morwen gave him a cool smile. "Isn't that what we are doing?"

That earned her a cold stare and a lengthening silence, broken when Thanda said, "I rescind Kronik's restrictions. You may visit your parent's house, sit at the table where they ate their meals, lie on the bed in which you were conceived — yes, I checked the records; your mother was pregnant when the raid came."

"Thank you," Morwen said.

Thanda said, "I am not without sentiment. Make your visit and we will talk again."

"I will."

He added, in a commanding tone, "But you will stay away from the maunch crop that grows nearby. If you show the slightest interest in the crop, its logistics, or those who handle it, I will consider you confirmed as an IPCC weasel."

Morwen made to reply, but Thanda spoke over her. "You will be tortured, killed, and dismembered. Your body parts will be freeze-dried and shipped to the nearest IPCC bureau."

"Understood," Morwen said.

Thanda had one last piece of information to impart. "Like the two that came before you."

With that, he turned and left the restaurant. The bell above the door jangled. Even after it stopped moving, the chime of its last note rang in the silence, fading slowly as Gisby, Terelia, and Morwen stood motionless.

Terelia brought a pot of hot punge over to the table where her husband and Morwen sat. She poured three mugs full and sat. Gisby took up his, and his hand shook so much that some of the brown liquid slopped over the top and stained the tablecloth. He used his other hand to steady the first and took a sip. Then he put down the mug and began to stir a spoon loudly.

Terelia said, quietly, "There are some things you need to know."

Morwen said, "Everywhere I go, people ask me questions about where I come from, why I'm here. I assume that Scrutineer Kronik has passed the word and everyone is reporting to him."

"That's normal," Gisby said. "Having Thanda come in here is not."

"He's got his own cook up at the Manse," Terelia said. "He's interested in you."

Morwen reached for her own mug. Its heat when she touched it made her realize that her hands were icy cold.

Morwen knew the place she was referring to. In her parents' time it had been a hotel, run as a source of revenue by the aristocrat who brought the first colonists to this world. The lordling had been killed resisting the assault. His guests and staff had all been taken offworld, except for those who were killed when they tried to defend their employer.

"Thanda wanted a secure room to store the extract," Gisby was saying. When he saw the term had no meaning to Morwen, he said, "We chew the maunch as a sacrament. It slowly opens the way to the sight-seeing. But Thanda developed a way of condensing the sacred element into a liquid. People who imbibe it…well, it seems they experience something different. None of us has ever tried it."

"He sells it to offworld criminals," Terelia said. "The proceeds are supposed to benefit the community — there's a formal Covenant — and to some extent they do, but…"

Gisby waved his free hand in a gesture that stopped his wife while he continued to stir loudly. He leaned toward Morwen and whispered, "There are listening devices. We've never found one here, but we've never really looked. It's a place where people meet and talk, so…"

Morwen nodded. Hacheem Belloch's overseers had used the same techniques to watch for sedition among his bondspeople.

Gisby continued to stir and whispered again, "You're not the first sojourner to come through New Dispensation and catch Thanda's eye. They were taken to the Manse and…"

Clink, clink, clink, went the spoon while Gisby's face silently finished the sentence.

Morwen lowered her voice. "I'm not interested in maunch or in the extract. I just wanted to be where my parents were."

It wasn't entirely true, but in Hacheem Belloch's house she had learned to be adept at lying. Honesty was a luxury slaves could rarely afford.

Terelia looked at the chronometer on the wall. "We need to get ready for lunch."

They swallowed their drinks and Morwen carried the mugs to the kitchen. As she passed Terelia, the woman whispered, "Just be careful."

• • •

That afternoon, in the slack-time between after-lunch clean-up and pre-dinner prep, Morwen went down Broadway to Credasper Street, and entered an establishment that sold goods that were useful for farm work. She asked the proprietor, who turned out to be the Palu Gurber of the compelling visions, if he had any heavy gloves: "Things that I could use when taking hot dishes out of an oven."

"Gisby is not well equipped?" Gurber said.

"He is, but I am the kind who likes to minimize risk."

The man went to a wall unit of small and medium-sized drawers, each with an enameled pull. He ran a finger along one horizontal row, went down two, and pulled open a drawer, from which he extracted a pair of heavy canvas gloves. The palms were reinforced with strips of thick leather.

"Blacksmiths use these," the man said. "Might be a little big for your hands."

Morwen tried them on, pronounced them suitable, and paid the price. Then she had to linger for a few minutes while the storekeeper made a clumsy attempt to engage her in conversation about her background and future plans. Morwen responded with the same bland history and prospects that had become her standard response to Kronik's informal interrogators.

Finally, she broke away. As she opened the door to depart, a vehicle approached, passing along Credasper Street. She recognized it. She also recognized the driver: Tosh Hubbley, the man who had given her a lift to the hotel by the crossroads. Her stepping out onto the pavement caught his eye and he turned his head to look at her. But his face showed no recognition. He faced forward again and drove on to the next cross street, turned south, and disappeared from view.

Back at the restaurant, she put the gloves into the cupboard in her room. Then she lay on the bed and looked at the flaking paint on the ceiling without seeing it, while her mind weighed and sifted what she had learned.

Thanda's visit had made it plain she was a person under observation. It would be strange if, having been given leave to visit her parents' old home, she did not take advantage of the opportunity. So, on Fifthday, after breakfast, she asked her employers for permission to skip clean-up and go up to the white house with the blasted tree.

"Go," said Terelia, while Gisby made brushing motions toward the door.

It was a mild morning, the world's yellow star pouring down soft light through a thin haze high in the sky. An errant breeze stirred Morwen's light skirt about her legs as she climbed the gentle slope of the first switchback. She thought about her parents making this climb, time and again — the house had been theirs since their arrival in Mount Pleasant — going to and from the restaurant.

A dusty lane met the fourth switchback at about its midpoint, where the slope leveled off into a terrace that widened toward the house. Plainly, Morwen saw, the flat space had been manufactured, a wall of fieldstone having been built, then tons of earth brought in to fill the gap between wall and natural slope. It had been built, her parents said, as a revenue house for one of the original settlers. The lane continued past the house to a group of greenhouses, from which Morwen was determined to keep her distance.

As she passed the lightning-struck tree, Morwen gave it a curious glance, but did not stop to examine it further. Thanda had directed her here, and her employers had told her about surveillance devices. It was not unreasonable to assume that she would be under observation. She would be expected to let curiosity and sentiment lead her into her parents' old home.

She noticed an outbuilding, the kind that might house a vehicle, but went past it to the front steps of the house. The wood was cracked with age and weathering, its red paint long since scoured away by wind, rain, and hail. The walls of the house showed peeled patches of white paint, with gray siding underneath. The windows were intact, but thick with grime.

The solid front door was not locked, but the hinges were stiff with rust. Morwen shouldered her way into a dimly lit living room, with a rug that was gray with twenty-some years' accumulation of dust and furniture similarly frosted with age. There were cobwebs in the ceiling corners and in the window frames.

Something indistinct was on the cushion of an armchair in one corner. Morwen thought it an item of discarded clothing, but when she came closer she saw that it was the mummified corpse of a cat.

"Mumpsimus," she said to herself. Her mother had often wondered if the pet had survived the loss of her caregiver. Now, one mystery was solved. "Poor thing," Morwen said, both because the sight of the poor, starved relic brought up a welling of sympathy, and because she was assuming Thanda had some kind of surveillance — sound at least, and perhaps visual as well — inside the house.

She passed through to the kitchen. Again, more dust. If the Dispers, upon arrival, had come to investigate the house, they hadn't disturbed much. Some drawers were opened and there were scuff marks of footprints in the floor's dust. On the window sill was a small ceramic, yellow flowers grouped in a dark blue vase. Morwen's father, courting her mother, had won it for her at a pitch-n-toss booth of a traveling fair that used to stop every autumn in the town where they lived on the Oikumene world of New Bruges, before they came to Providence and Mount Pleasant.

Morwen picked it up, dusted it with a cloth she found tucked into the handle of a drawer, and brought it close for inspection. She fought down the emotion — mingled sadness and hopelessness — that tried to take charge of her.

Never give in. Push on and endure, said her father's voice, the words she had been hearing since childhood. She tucked the little gimcrack in the pocket of her skirt, took a last look at the kitchen, and found the back stairs that led to the upper story.

Her parents' bedroom was plain: a double bed covered neatly with a patterned quilt, an armoire with a few changes of clothes, two bedside tables, one with a dead clock, the other with a lamp and a paper-covered book. Morwen picked it up, saw a bookmark, and opened it to the marked page.

Veddo came down to the village from the hills, she read silently, *carrying the sword and shield he had wrested from Garjan the Cruel. The villagers turned out to see him, but he rode straight to Brodo the headman's house, where Brodo's daughter, the fair Morwen, waited.*

Morwen read that last sentence again. Now she knew where her name came from. Tears welled up, but she fought them. Falling victim to sentiment would not help. She put the book back and went out into the hall and along to the second bedroom. This was unfurnished, except for an infant's crib, painted wood adorned with representations of anthropomorphic animals engaged in comic activities.

Nothing else was in the room that would have been Morwen's. Her mother's pregnancy had been confirmed just days before the Demon Princes descended to turn happy expectation into decades of misery.

But not despair, Morwen told herself. *Never give in. Push on and endure.*

She went back downstairs and out the front door. The outbuilding drew her attention now. Its doors, one large, one small, were locked, but she cleared the grime from a window and peered in. She saw no vehicle; her parents had been saving for the birth and the distance between home and work was not great.

But was there something in a corner? Morwen hunted around, saw a line of rocks at the side of the house. They marked a flower bed, now overgrown with weeds. She got one and brought it back to the outbuilding. It was a choice between smashing a window or a lock, and she realized the latter, rusted to uselessness, was the obvious choice. She hammered the keyhole on the smaller door until the old wood of the jamb gave way. Then she shoved the door ajar and entered.

With the door open, more light penetrated, and Morwen saw that the thing in the corner was an electrically-assisted bicycle. Her parents had never mentioned it. When she stood it up for an examination, she saw why: loose wires and a missing photocell. The thing was broken.

And yet it might be mended. There was a man in town, Bod Hipple, who repaired broken farm machinery. He might be able to repair this. And he was quite taken with Morwen's fritters. Or perhaps with their maker. She'd seen how his eyes followed her when he came to The Eatery.

She wheeled the bike out on its flat tires, pulled the door shut, then was stopped by a thought. She stepped back into the shed, picked up a shovel she had seen leaning in a corner, and dug a hole in what had been her mother's flower bed. She went into the house, wrapped the mummified cat in a towel, brought it out, and buried it.

Then she returned the shovel to the shed, stood the bike upright, and walked it back to town.

• • •

After lunch and clean-up, Morwen went up to her room, lay on the bed, and thought about her parents' house. She thought about things she had seen — scuff marks on floors, a torn spider's web in a corner of the living room — and what they meant. She had been careful not to peer directly, but she was reasonably sure that Jerz Thanda had sent his men to the house to plant surveillance devices that might reveal her as an IPCC weasel. They had left traces.

The fact that she was not a police secret agent did not reassure her. Thanda would err on the side of caution. If his suspicion tipped too far, he would not wait for certainty. He would act based on probabilities. She went into her little kitchen and drew a glass of water, sipped it while she looked about from the corners of her eyes. She spotted a tiny hole in the wall just below the ceiling. When she went back into the bedroom, she saw another.

She would have to accept that her privacy was erased. Thanda's operatives would watch her undress, stand under the ablutory's flow, use the toilet. And she would have to give no inkling that she was aware of being watched. Let a little time go by without raising the level of suspicion, and possibly the level of surveillance would abate. In the meantime, she would set her plan aside and just be a cook in a small-town restaurant.

She could do that. She had waited years for the fleeting opportunity to escape from Belloch's compound in Boregore, cross the sea, and stow away on a space-faring freighter. And when the opportunity came, she had been ready.

She lay back on the bed and looked at the little ceramic she had brought back from her mother's kitchen. It had waited more than twenty-five years for her to come and rescue it. She could learn patience from it.

After a while, she closed her eyes and slept.

Chapter Three

Jerz Thanda's drug extraction and shipping operations happened in plain sight. The first greenhouses where maunch was grown had been established by the Dispers as soon as they had settled in the ghost town of Mount Pleasant. These had been small affairs, sufficient to grow enough of the herb to meet the congregation's sacramental requirements.

In those days, and for years after, maunch-tending had been a minor part of the new community's life. Most Dispers were engaged in the characteristic pursuits of an agricultural society. They grew produce, tended livestock, maintained machinery, shot hoppers when they came onto their land, and practiced all the arts that sustained a reasonably civilized existence. Children went to school, the restaurant served meals, the roads were repaired in summer and plowed in winter, people pooled their talents and put on concerts and plays.

It was not a democracy. Their founder, Porleth Armbruch, called The Prophet, was an unquestioned leader. But he operated on the basis of consensus. If an issue needed to be decided, he would put it to the commonality. People would discuss pros and cons at impromptu debates in the old community hall after meet-ups or over meals at the restaurant, or anywhere Dispers might gather. Eventually, a common view would arise, leaving aside the opinions of a few outliers, and Armbruch would make a declaration.

Thus it went until the fateful day when the founder's vehicle had struck a fallen tree, laid in the road by a spring windstorm. Somehow the impact had broken Armbruch's neck, and Jerz Thanda had stepped into the vacancy. He was a recent convert to the Doctrine of the New

Dispensation who had arrived from Crickle, a medium-sized city ruled by criminal gangs on the southern shore of the northern continent. His life in Crickle, when it was investigated by Eldo Kronik, was a handful of generalities, but he quickly established himself as useful to The Prophet, encouraging the expansion of maunch growing and raising the prospect of selling the surplus to offworlders.

Before The Prophet's death, Thanda's ideas were outside the consensus. All that changed once he had control. Thanda saw maunch-growing as a missed opportunity. The active psychostimulant, he was sure, could be extracted and concentrated. It would have value on many worlds in the Beyond, and even in the Oikumene. The Disper community needed to be reoriented, so that extract production and sale would become the prime focus.

When this new strategy was announced, the normal process of debate and discussion began. But it was swiftly truncated by a group of men that Thanda had formed about him, some of them also recent arrivals from Crickle. They were rarely seen at the meet-ups, and it was thought they only attended to keep an eye on the commonality.

None of them took the sacrament, so they did not acquire the personality aspects that regular maunch-chewing encouraged: placidity, equanimity, otherworldliness, and a tendency not to fret about life's vicissitudes.

Thanda's men — the Protectors, they called themselves — closed down debates by shouting and creating a hurly-burly. They were not averse to pushing and tripping, and somehow their knees and elbows made contact with farmers and school teachers and tractor repairmen, leaving bruises and the implied threat of worse.

Some individuals stood up to them. These champions received private visits from the Protectors at their homes. One particularly outspoken farmer, Lock Guysek, somehow managed to fall from his hayloft onto a disk harrow. He died of blood loss before his wife found him.

After that, the life of New Dispensation went on much as before, except that teams of men were conscripted to build an extraction mill next to the great stone house where Thanda and his Protectors had installed themselves. Several new greenhouses were built and seeded, followed by several more. Farmers who had formerly concerned themselves with raising their own crops and animals now found themselves working under a corvee system, one day out of seven, to tend, harvest, and transport the huge new quantities of maunch to the mill.

Then it became two days, then three. But the mill was buying all the maunch the farmers could grow, and at a good price. After the first offworld sales of extract, Thanda began to pay the corvee conscripts a generous wage. Luxuries that previously had been beyond the reach of New Dispensation began to flow into the community from Hambledon's spaceport. There were still some grumbles, but most accepted the situation as workable.

The mill's output, in small vials closely packed in straw-filled crates, was not handled by the commonality. Nor was its transportation to Hambledon contracted to the local farmers who shipped the raw maunch for twenty percent of the proceeds. Instead, Thanda's Protectors escorted the extract to Hambledon, guarding it closely until it was loaded onto vessels with disabled transponders that would carry it out into the immensity.

Thanda spent a good portion of the revenue generated by the extract trade on benefits to the community, but it was speculated that most of the funds remained under Thanda's control. It was speculated, not known for certain, because anyone who raised the subject was met with instant discouragement. Lock Guysek's demise was not forgotten.

All this Morwen learned as her time in New Dispensation extended into weeks. She had quiet conversations with Gisby and Terelia, outside of the restaurant when they would tour various farms to purchase produce and meat. She also talked to Bod Hipple, the man who repaired her electric bike and refused to take more than five SVU for his work. Morwen had a growing sense that the bachelor mechanic was developing "sweetlings" for her, as the Dispers called such emotions. An invitation to some personal encounter seemed to be in the offing.

Morwen was not attracted to Bod Hipple. He was large and ungainly, his face broad and red and his ears protruding like two small flags. She believed he had first taken an interest in her when Kronik had put out the word to the community, but now he had fixed on her as a potential "intended," as the Dispers called such a relationship.

Morwen felt some qualms about leading the fellow on, but she had a task to perform on Providence that had been set for her by her parents when she was a little girl. She meant to see it through. She would deal with any regrets and remorse once her mother and father were free.

Patience was what the situation required, Morwen reminded herself daily. She immersed herself in the routines of work and allowed herself to be coaxed by her employers into attending the Firstday meet-ups at the Dispers' temple. She also went to an evening concert of vocal music at the same location, and applauded politely the relatively tuneful renditions of a female duet, a four-man ensemble that achieved some interesting effects with contrapuntal harmonies, and a final singalong that involved all in attendance, including her.

She even allowed herself to be escorted to a dance featuring a visiting quartet from Hambledon. The steps were new to her, but her escort, the freshly shaved and tight-collared Bod Hipple, instructed her in the complexities. Flushed and somewhat breathless after the exertions of the evening, she allowed the repairman to walk her home and rewarded him with a kiss on the cheek at the bottom of the stairs.

Morwen was not greatly experienced in courtship. Her owner had discouraged his slaves from forming their own relationships. He bred them according to his own interests, often selling the infants to other slavers. The bereft parents were also discouraged from asking what happened to their children. So she was not skilled in reading the ambitions of a suitor. Still, when she allowed Hipple her cheek then drew away, she saw his pupils widen despite their being lit only by the dim glow from a distant streetlight. For a moment, she thought she saw the same feral gleam she had seen in the eyes of the captain of the *Festerlein*.

She climbed the stairs, went inside, and locked the door.

She had not got much use out of the bike, but she did pedal it up to her parents' house, the electric motor amplifying her efforts on the switchbacks. She opened her parents' closets, finding much of the clothing had become food for insects. But there were several cotton dresses of her mother's and these she loaded into a basket that Bod had fastened to the front of the vehicle and brought them down to her apartment. She also brought the book her mother had been reading.

• • •

Weeks went by. When Morwen judged the time was right, she went after lunch to the constabulary and asked to see Senior Scrutineer Kronik. He received her in his sparsely furnished, second-floor office at the rear of the building, with a view of her parents' house and the great stone pile of Jerz Thanda's Manse high above it. His questioning look invited her to state her business.

"My parents' old house," she said. "Does it belong to anyone?"

"It belongs to the community of New Dispensation. Why?"

She answered his question with another of her own. "Would anyone mind if I lived there?"

His face was built for skepticism. "Without electricity?"

"Could it not be reconnected?"

He conceded the possibility. "Why do you wish to live there?"

"I miss my father and my mother. I feel closer to them there."

He looked at the flower-printed dress she was wearing. "Was that your mother's?"

"Yes."

"It does not bother you that it is years out of style?"

"Obviously not," she said.

He studied her silently for several heartbeats. "You cannot own the property, not being a member of the commune. But as a sojourner, you may rent it. You will have to pay for power and water."

"There is a well and a pump," she said.

"It is still the commune's water."

She raised her hands to show her side of the argument was over. "Who will establish the rates?"

"The commune. In effect, me." He pulled a pad of paper toward him on the desktop and reached for a stylus. "I will calculate and let you know."

She thanked him and left. Later that day, a junior scrutineer came to the restaurant and presented her with a document defining her as the property's tenant. It specified the amount of the rent and the fees for water and energy. There was also a nominal charge for use of the bicycle, back-dated to the day she had wheeled it down the hill.

The house's mop was eaten away by mold and rot, but the rest of the cleaning gear was still usable. Morwen began to devote her evenings to making the house livable, sweeping, dusting, beating rugs and furniture in the front yard to raise clouds of gray powder that blew away on the breeze. On her second bout, Terelia came with her, and together they stripped the old bed to wash the sheets and quilt. Generations of mice had colonized the mattress, so they took it outside, chased away the small, gray invaders, and burnt the well holed pad.

The machine that cleaned fabrics still worked, once its power source was reestablished, though the blue sparks that first accompanied its electrostatic functioning were an initial worry when they tested it on a pillow case. But once it quieted down, they loaded in the sheets, setting aside the quilt for its own turn.

While the device was crackling and humming, Terelia said, "Gisby and I are sad to lose you. We liked hearing you walking around up there. It was like having a daughter."

Morwen was not sure how to respond, but the woman filled the awkward silence. "I suppose you'll now be able to entertain Bod Hipple… properly."

Morwen's reply was careful. "I'm not sure I want to…'entertain' Bod."

Terelia cocked her head. "He's pretty sure he wants to be entertained. He's told some of his cronies he means to make you his intended."

Again, Morwen thought it wise to remain silent. Bod Hipple did not figure in her long-term plans. What his plans were also remained unspoken, although the mores of the Dispers were lenient in regard to relations between the sexes.

It took several days to cleanse the house thoroughly, until the hardwood floors gleamed with wax and the windows were crystal clear. The curtains, once shaken out and cleaned, were a cheerfully bright blue. Morwen bought paint from Palu Gurber and did the kitchen walls in a warm shade of yellow-gold, with white for the trim, which Terelia said made her feel she was standing amid scrambled eggs.

Bod came by to examine all the household machinery, especially the well pump. He made some adjustments and applied lubricants and now some of the background noises were diminished. Morwen rewarded him by opening a bottle of meadwine brought in from Hambledon, and they sat on the edge of the porch watching Providence's star descend behind the western hills.

Their conversation was sparse, Bod not being of a loquacious type, but the silences were not uncomfortable. Morwen had a sense that the shy mechanic was working his way up to some crescendo. She forestalled it by indicating a heavy vehicle that was making its way up the switchbacks, past her house and on to the stone structure where Jerz Thanda and his Protectors lived.

"That's the fourth or fifth truck like that I've seen going up the past few days," she said.

Bod Hipple looked around, though they were quite solitary, then spoke softly. "They're building something up there."

"What?"

He sighed and let his shoulders rise and fall. "Nobody told me, and I got the feeling I shouldn't ask. Just fix the compressor and get back down the hill."

"But you didn't need to ask, did you?" Morwen said.

He shook his head. "It's a concrete pad, wide and thick, with runnels lined with high-temperature ceramics running from the center to the edges."

Morwen had seen plenty of those. She kept her voice low. "They're going to land space ships."

"Uh-huh."

"But Hambledon spaceport is only a couple of hours away, and it has no import-export controls."

Bod looked around again, then put his lips close to her ear and whispered, "Weasels."

From then on, he showed discomfort and asked her not to say anything, not even to Gisby and Terelia. "If it got to —" he cocked his head to indicate uphill "— you-know-who that I'd said something... well, you know..."

"I know," Morwen said. "Thanda won't hear anything from me."

On the first of the month of Cinquomese, Morwen went to the town hall to pay her rent and rates, counting out the svu to a bored clerk. That done, she went to the rear of the building and up the stairs to Kronik's office. His door was open and she saw him standing at the window, fists on his hips, staring at Thanda's residence.

She coughed in the doorway to get his attention and he spun round, a hard expression on his face that softened only to neutral at the sight of her. "What do you want?"

"I wanted to thank you for letting me have the house. It means a lot to me."

He returned her look with a blank stare, then said, "You're welcome, but your happiness is scarcely my concern."

"All right." She turned to leave then looked back at him. "Have you decided I'm not a weasel?" she said.

He showed a half-smile. "In the Beyond, every sojourner is potentially a weasel," he said, "but let us say your potentiality has diminished."

"Then I will continue to tread softly," Morwen said.

Kronik looked away from her to the great stone house atop the hill. "I would advise it," he said.

While cleaning, Morwen had checked to see if the surveillance pickups were still in place. The ones she had originally identified no longer were, but it was possible that others had been installed now that the place was habitable. With the house's various devices restored to functionality, there was every possibility Kronik was keeping tabs on her for Jerz Thanda.

Her presence on the hill leading to the Protectors' headquarters was surely grounds for suspicion, but it could not be helped. It was where the lightning-struck oak stood, and she had come lightyears across space to find that tree.

She had taken to walking out to the tree in the evenings, first having manufactured a plausible excuse to do so. Providence had no bird species of its own, and none that had been transplanted here had survived. They had fallen prey to the flitter-byes, rat-sized, web-winged creatures with sharp teeth and claws that fed on flying insectoids and anything small that crawled in plain sight. They had eaten the nestlings of avians transplanted from several worlds.

So, there was no birdsong on Providence, but the flitter-byes were valued for their work in keeping down swarms of blood-hunting spikles, four-winged flyers a finger-joint in length whose bites caused pain and could carry disease from one person to another.

To encourage flitter-byes to control the insectoid pests around human habitation, people hung wooden houses from porch rafters and nearby trees. Morwen had bought one and hung it in the lower branches of the blasted oak, quite near to a hole in the trunk. Every evening, as dark settled, she would go out to the tree and leave some kitchen scraps in the hollow where a large branch sprang from the bole, to draw flitter-byes to the tree, so that they might decide to make it their base.

It became a ritual. Anyone who was observing her would find nothing untoward in her doing what many inhabitants of New Dispensation, and indeed all over temperate-climate Providence, did daily.

"Bod," she said, softly, at the same time stirring his cup of brew for him, "do you know a man named Hubbley?"

He looked up at her, where she stood behind the counter. "The Traffard sales rep? Sure. I buy supplies from him." His brows drew down. "Do *you* know him?"

"He gave me a ride from Hambledon spaceport when I was coming here. I thought I saw him again, the other day."

Bod's face cleared. "He comes by every ten days. Seems pretty crisp, for an outsider," he said, using a local word for acceptable. Morwen hadn't asked for the derivation, but believed it came from the varied textures of maunch when it was chewed for meet-ups. A crisp and crunchy mouthful was preferred.

She stopped stirring and set the spoon aside. "What about me?" she said. "Am I considered 'crisp'?"

He gave a half-chuckle. "You're getting there."

She moved the conversation on, mentioning the dance planned for Fifthday in a way that left open an invitation to invite. Bod took it.

The dance came and went, the only item of note being that Maddie, the serving woman from Brumble's, came up with a party of young folks from the farms surrounding New Dispensation. They were well received, dancing with Dispers amiably, although the local steps differed from those the Dispers had brought from offworld.

Morwen approached Maddie during an interval, when the band

stepped down from the stage to drink ale and stand outside in the cool evening air.

"Interesting dress," Maddie said, eying Morwen's cotton print.

"My mother's."

The young woman's brows rose. "And thereby hangs a tale," she said.

Morwen told her what she had told others. Maddie listened, then said, "I thought you had more on your mind than idle curiosity."

"Would you like your clothes back?" Morwen said.

"Just that vest." Maddie indicated the ensemble she was wearing: a gold knee-length dress over textured stockings and patent leather pumps. "It goes well with this."

"I could go and get it."

"Bring it to the next dance."

Another week passed. Morwen was increasingly sure the surveillance devices had been removed. Perhaps Kronik had better things for his constables to do. She continued her routines, nonetheless, though one evening she took the blacksmith's gloves out to the flitter-byes' house so that her hands were protected when she lifted the little box from its hanger, unlatched the lid, and cleaned out its inner space.

Afterward, she left the gloves at the foot of the tree, rehung the shelter, and went back to her parents' house. She sat on the porch and drank a glass of meadwine, another element of her daily routine. Then she went to bed.

More days passed without incident, except that Morwen kept an eye on Broadway whenever work at the restaurant allowed her to watch passing vehicles. The day came when she saw Tosh Hubbley's carryall pass by, and she made a mental note of the date and hour. Ten days later, at about the same time in the afternoon, she saw him drive by again.

In between those appearances, she worked, kept house, went to Firstday meetings with Gisby and Terelia — though she did not accede to their gentle suggestions that she chew the maunch — and attended another Fifthday dance, escorted by Bod Hipple. She sensed that he was becoming more comfortable in her presence, but that sense of security seemed to be edging over into an air of possessiveness.

When she brought along Maddie's brocaded vest, he asked her about it as they walked along Broadway toward the meeting house.

"It belongs to a friend," Morwen said. "I'm returning it."

"What friend?" he said. "You don't know anybody here."

"Someone I met on the way to New Diss. She lent me clothes so I wouldn't stand out like a black tooth."

Hipple's face showed a struggle between confusion and disapproval. The latter won out. "Not good to get close to outsiders," he said.

"Really?" Morwen said. "You have."

With that, she quickened her pace and stepped away from him. "Wait!" he called after her, but she didn't. She passed through the playground equipment outside the community hall, tripped up the concrete stairs, and walked into the dance just as the band finished tuning up and launched into Shanker's Trot, a lively tune.

Morwen slipped on Maddie's vest, approached the nearest knot of young, male Dispers, and selected the first one who met her gaze. Moments later, they were out on the floor, performing the kickstep. As she twirled, she saw Hipple glowering in the doorway. Then she caught sight of Maddie with her out-of-town friends. Morwen flicked the collar of the vest to draw attention to it, and the other woman nodded.

When Shanker's Trot ended with a clash of cymbals, Morwen found Maddie and slipped off the vest. Maddie put it on, leaving the loops unfastened.

"You're right," Morwen said. "It goes well with that outfit."

She turned and saw Hipple across the floor. He was still glowering.

The days wore on. Bod Hipple didn't come to the restaurant for a while after they had separated at the dance. Morwen wondered if he thought she should seek him out and mollify him. She raised the issue with Terelia.

"Let it lie," the older woman said. "Bod Hipple has delusions of self-worth. It will do him good to let a little air out of him."

More time passed, and Morwen watched for Tosh Hubbley. *Patience*, she told herself.

Her expectations were rewarded, ten days after his last appearance, by a repetition of the man's visit to town. Nine days after that, in the deepening dark of evening, Morwen went out to the flitter-byes' house again, put on the gloves lying on the ground, cleaned the little shelter, and put in a few scraps of meat left over from her dinner.

She rehung the house, then stepped halfway around the tree, and put a gloved hand into the hole in the trunk. She felt something move against her covered palm and closed her fingers on it. She lifted her hand out of the cavity and saw, in the dim light of dusk, something squirming to free itself from her grasp.

Stingtails, said her father's voice in her head. *Always a nest of them. Wear heavy gloves.*

Morwen turned and threw the segmented creature toward where the level terrace ended and the downslope began. She reached again into the hole, felt around, but encountered no more denizens. The creatures were known to go out at sundown, to hunt in the grass for the scent trails of small, warm-blooded creatures. Stingtails were particularly drawn to the odor of lactating females, which they followed into their burrows, where they stung and carried off the young.

Morwen dug deep, finding the bottom of the hole filled with tiny skulls and ribcages, as well as the shed exoskeletons of the creatures that had fed on the captive flesh. The gloves made it difficult to determine what she was touching, and she did not want to spread the detritus around the base of the tree.

Finally, she determined that no stingtail remained in the nest. She removed a glove and reached in again, her fingers digging through the bones and chitin. The hole was deep, and she had to insert her full arm before her fingertips brushed against something small, hard, and round. She shoved deeper, paining her armpit, and was at last able to scoop the object into her palm.

She closed her finger about it and drew it out, slipping it immediately into a pocket on the front of her dress. Then she turned toward the house. She calculated that it had taken only moments to complete the operation, and she had done so with the bole of the oak between her and the house. If there were any devices spying on her, she should have been safe from view. Or maybe the watcher sitting in front of the screens might have looked away, reaching for a cup of brew, for those few seconds while she acted out her regular evening routine.

Time would tell. She resumed her seat upon the porch and took up a glass of meadwine. She hoped that no sensor was measuring her heart rate, with her pulse pounding in her ears.

After a while she took the glass indoors, rinsed it, and put it away. She went to the bedroom that had been her parents', undressed, and got under the covers. She had palmed the object from the tree, and now she felt its spherical surface, crossed with faintly incised lines.

She had come a long way to find it. She still had a long way to go.

Tosh Hubbley came every tenth day. On the day after she retrieved the object from the blasted tree, Morwen packed her ditty bag with some small clothes, her spacer's garb, and the flowery knick-knack from her parents' courtship. She put the bag in the bike's basket and tamped it down so it would not be too noticeable. Then she rode down the switchbacks into town and reported for work.

It was a normal morning, followed by a normal lunch. A few days before, Bod Hipple had resumed coming for lunch. Today, he lingered over a cup of punge, talking to her as she helped clear the tables. She asked him how his afternoon looked and he told her he was working on a couple of maunch harvesters that were near the end of their mechanical lifespan.

"And that Traffard rep is bringing me some parts I need." Morwen said nothing. Bod continued, in a tone of diffident hope, "Could we take a walk together after supper?"

"I guess so." she said.

"I want to ask you something."

She felt a pang of guilt, but forced it away. "All right."

After lunch clean-up, Gisby and Terelia went home for a nap. By the way he put his hand on her lower back as they went out the door, Morwen thought there might be more than sleeping involved.

After that, she waited by the window, watching the street. It seemed a long time before Tosh Hubbley's carryall drove by. She then forced herself to wait longer, and had to resist the temptation to put her hand into her dress pocket, to feel the small, round thing beneath her crumpled handkerchief.

Finally, she left the restaurant, locking the door behind her, and mounted her bicycle. She rode sedately along Broadway then turned onto Credasper. The carryall was nosed into the curb in front of Bod's premises. She stopped, pulled her bike onto the sidewalk, and waited.

It seemed forever, but then she saw Hubbley exit the repair shop, fold a piece of paper that he tucked into a pocket, and get into the vehicle. It started up, backed into the street, and began to head downhill, to where the ring road ran toward the broad thoroughfare that led out of town.

Morwen pushed the bike onto the road, pedaled, then engaged the electric motor that amplified the power of her feet. The bike picked up speed, her hair blowing back from her face.

As she passed Bod Hipple's business, he came out of the door. She saw surprise on his face and heard him call her name, but she did not look back. Hubbley's carryall was nearly to the turn onto the ring road. Morwen pedaled faster, and the bike's semi-sentient circuitry took the hint. She was going fast now.

Hubbley slowed as he approached the turn, where traffic rules called for a stop before proceeding. Morwen caught up with him just as he stopped and began to move again toward the road that led to the bridge, then on to the highway that ran to Hambledon. She passed him, cut in front of him, and squeezed hard on her bike's brake levers, causing the bike to slew sideways in his path.

She saw his face register shock as he stepped hard on the carryall's braking pedal and turned the wheel sharply. For a moment she feared the vehicle would topple sideways and crush her, but it came to a shuddering stop, rocking on its suspension.

A long moment passed, then Hubbley opened the driver's door and stepped out, to regard her with astonishment. "What was that all about?" he said.

"I need a ride. Out of town."

He was still having difficulty fathoming what was happening. "Take the omnibus," he said.

"Can't. They watch it. I need to go, and I need to go now."

"What have you done?" he said.

She waved away the question. "No time for that."

He studied her and she saw the shock fade as his mind started working again. "You're a weasel."

"I am not."

"Then why are you running?"

"Another reason. Let's go."

A siren sounded from the town. "Too late," he said.

Morwen felt an upwelling of despair. "No," she said. She looked at her bike, its handles still grasped in her hands, then at Hubbley's carryall.

He shut the driver's door and leaned against it. "No. They'll run you down." He glanced around at the fields. "If the hoppers don't get you."

A black ground car was coming down the hill toward them, its siren wailing and the lights on its roof and grill flashing. It slowed as it reached the carryall, passed Hubbley and Morwen, then turned sideways to block the road.

Kronik got out of the passenger seat. Three of his deputies exited through the other doors. One carried a long-barreled disorganizer. Kronik and the others each placed a hand on their holstered sidearms.

"What's going on?" Kronik said.

Morwen stood silent, her gaze on the road. Hubbley showed his hands far from his body and said, "I don't really know."

The scrutineer looked from Hubbley to Morwen and back again. "What's your relationship with this woman?"

"I gave her a lift once, from Hambledon to Brumble's hotel."

"That's it?"

"That's it. I haven't seen her since."

A second black car pulled up behind the carryall. Two of Thanda's Protectors got out. The big one with carrot-colored hair and red ears said, "We'll take this."

Kronik stiffened. His three deputies switched their attention to the new arrivals. "This is my jurisdiction," Kronik said. "I'll handle it."

"She's a weasel," the Protector said.

"No," said Kronik, "she is not." He gave Morwen a considering look. "Just what she is, I don't know yet. But I mean to find out."

"Give her to us," said the big-eared Protector. His freckled face was flushed with red.

"No," said Kronik. He undid the flap of his holster. Two of his deputies did the same, while the third thumbed a stud on the disorganizer. Its hum as it cycled up to active status was loud in the silence.

"You'll regret this," said the Protector.

"I'll add it to the list of things I regret," said Kronik.

Thanda's man said something under his breath, then he and the other Protector got into their car, reversed in a three-point turn and drove back up toward the town.

"You'll come with us," Kronik said to Morwen. He glanced after the departing car. "You wouldn't like the alternative."

They didn't take Hubbley, too. Morwen rode in the rear of the scrutineer's car, wedged between two of the deputies. They'd put her bike in the luggage compartment. They parked behind the town hall and climbed an outside staircase to the constabulary offices. Kronik and one of the deputies led her to an interrogation room and told her to sit. It was a repetition of her first interview, but today the atmosphere was different. She clasped her hands in her lap to disguise their trembling.

"Why not just take the omnibus?" Kronik said.

"Your men watch it. You'd have stopped me."

Kronik blew out his cheeks. "We might have asked where you were going, but we had no grounds to detain you."

The answer confused Morwen. "You'd think I was a weasel."

"I know you're not," Kronik said. "Just exactly what you are and what you've been doing, that's been a minor mystery."

He paused to allow Morwen to say something. She did not.

He continued, "But I've seen nothing to make me think you're a danger to the people I protect." He paused again, then added, "Except to Bod Hipple's sentimental heart."

"He called you."

"He did. I'm afraid he's not pleased with you."

Another deputy came into the room and placed Morwen's ditty bag on the table. Kronik pulled it toward him, loosened the draw string, and began to empty its contents.

He brought out Morwen's spacer costume. "Well," he said, "that answers the question of where you were going. Planning to loiter around the spaceport until you landed a berth?"

Morwen nodded.

He unfolded an undershirt wrapped around something solid and found the little ceramic pot with its burst of yellow flowers. He rotated the item in his hands and studied it closely. "Ahah," he said, softly, then gave her an amused look. "Evidence," he said.

Morwen's voice was sharp and defensive. "That was my mother's!"

"I believe you," Kronik said. "In fact, it confirms what we've been able to discover about you."

Now he had Morwen off-balance. "What are you talking about?"

Kronik put the ceramic on the table and leaned back in his chair. "Your parents were Chaffe and Elva Sabine," he said. "Their records are still in the building. That's how we knew the house was theirs. Also the bike, by the way."

He reached out a finger and touched one of the little blossoms. "We have their medical records, including the results of the pregnancy test. We have the license they acquired to operate a restaurant and the health inspector's reports — very commendable."

Kronik showed her a knowing smile. Morwen knew he was building up to something. She waited for it, and now it came.

"We also have the forms they filled in when they first arrived in Mount Pleasant, noting their place of origin and the name of the ship that brought them to Providence."

He picked up the ceramic and turned it over, showing her a small lozenge painted onto the base. "That's the mark of the Voorheft Pottery, located in the city of Loomers on the world New Bruges."

He paused again, for effect. "New Bruges is in the Oikumene. That's where your parents came from. And my guess is they were on the run. Oikumeners consider us Beyonders a rabble of barbarians. Nobody leaves the Oikumene for the Beyond unless they're fleeing trouble. Or looking for it."

Morwen said nothing.

"I sent Scrutineer Toba to Loomers," Kronik said. "She's good at finding out things. Our version of a weasel, in fact.

"She found an interesting story in a publication called *Extant*. About two criminal families who were contesting for the right — no, let's call it the power — to control illicit activities in Loomers.

"After the usual preliminaries in dark alleys and seedy restaurants, one family, the Horths, staged a full-scale raid on the house where lived

Purpuram Gratz, head of the Gratz crime family. There was blood and violence, and Master Purpuram and his senior henchmen got the worst of it."

He paused again and said, "Does any of this sound familiar?"

Morwen saw there was no point denying it. Kronik and his fact-sifting deputy were good at their profession. She said, "My parents were not gangsters. They were just servants in the Gratzes' manor. He was the family's chef and she was a plaincook, his helper. When the Horths came, they fled."

Kronik's face showed that he had a point to make. "Fled all the way to the Beyond," he said. "Although no one should have been looking to harm the hired help."

He waited for her to respond, and when nothing was forthcoming, he said, "Unless, in all the chaos and hurly burly, the hired help helped themselves to something they shouldn't have."

He fixed Morwen with an inquisitive gaze. "Something small and valuable that, and I'm just guessing here, they hid somewhere on their rented property in the quiet backwater of Mount Pleasant."

He waited again, then grimaced and said, "From which they meant to move on, once the rumpus on New Bruges had died down. But their plans went awry when the Demon Princes descended on the town and scooped up the inhabitants.

"Chaffe and Elva Sabine found themselves carried off to the slave pens at Interchange, where they were lucky to be bought as a couple by...What was his name again?"

Morwen said, "Hacheem Belloch. And I would not call it lucky."

"I won't dispute that," Kronik said. He resumed his tale. "In Belloch's house they gave birth to a daughter, whom they trained to make her way across space to their old rented house and find whatever they stole from the Gratz family."

Morwen sighed. "But there was nothing there."

Kronik scoffed at that. "It was there, and once you had it, you ran. The question now is, what is it? And what are we going to do with it?"

"We?" she said.

"Whatever it is, it was abandoned by your parents —" he raised a hand to forestall her objection "— admittedly, unwillingly abandoned. But, then, its ownership was a gray area to begin with, wasn't it?"

Morwen said a short word, out of context in her present situation, but succinctly summing up her emotional state.

"It's not in here," Kronik said, touching the ditty bag. "That means it is on, possibly *in* your person. Shall I call in Toba to search you again, or will you give up the pretense and spare us all the unpleasantness?"

He interlaced his fingers and placed his hands on the tabletop, his expression saying he expected a response.

Morwen considered her options, found there actually were none. She reached into the pocket of her dress, pulled out her wadded hand-kerchief, and then produced a dark orb, about the size of her thumbnail. She placed the scrunched handkerchief on the table, then nestled the object in it so it could not roll away.

Kronik leaned forward, studied the thing for a while, then picked it up and examined it more closely.

"What is it?" he said.

Morwen said, "I don't know," which brought a a growl of exaspera-tion from the scrutineer. "I really don't," she said. "Neither did mom and dad. All they knew was that it was Master Gratz's most prized pos-session. He kept it in a secure room, locked in its own special case. All the servants speculated about what it might be. There was even a pool.

"My dad would never have gotten in there, except that the Horths had infiltrated the manor's defenses and they blew the power system, including the backups, before they came in shooting.

"My father ran upstairs, grabbed the...whatever it is, and he and my mother went out the rear service tunnel and ran for their lives."

Kronik regarded her. Eventually, she decided, he accepted her story as truth, which it was. He took another look at the small orb, rubbed it between forefinger and thumb, then said to his deputy, "Bring me a magnifier."

A device was brought, and Kronik positioned the orb under its aperture. He turned on the power, adjusted a control, then another. A screen appeared above the device, showing an image like the surface of a dark planet seen from near orbit. The darkness was crisscrossed by thin lines of light: silver, white, and electric blue, forming intricate patterns, whorls and arabesques, helixes and spirals.

"Huh," said Kronik. His face took on a thoughtful cast. "I believe I know what this is," he said. "An information storage device. You put it into the right reader and it disgorges what it knows." He examined the lines and colors. "But..."

"But what?" Morwen said.

He looked at her. "It will be encrypted in multiple layers and formats. The most powerful integrator at the Institute might be tasked with unraveling its defenses without knowing the key, but it would take decades to work through all the permutations and find the one that unlocks it." He turned off the magnifier. "But you already knew that."

Morwen made no reply.

Kronik waited a little more then said, "It might be a key, but you have to find the lock it fits. Or it might be a map to some place someone wanted hidden. Or it could be a bearer certificate for a billion SVU, or the deed that confers ownership of something worth owning.

"Whatever it is, a serious criminal in the Oikumene thought it was the most valuable thing he owned."

He took up the orb again, letting it rest in his palm. "We'll just have to find out," he said.

"I'll tell you what it is," Morwen said. "It's the thing that will buy my parents out of slavery."

Kronik frowned and opened his mouth to answer. But at that moment, the door to the room opened and Jerz Thanda stood in the doorway. He looked from Kronik to Morwen then back to the scrutineer.

"What's going on?" he said. Then his gaze went to the object in Kronik's open hand. "And what might that be?"

Chapter Four

Jerz Thanda was not happy with the explanation he was hearing from Kronik. He kept shaking his head as the scrutineer related what had been learned so far about the encrypted bead. Finally, he made a more forceful gesture.

"It's a diversion!" he shouted. "She's a weasel and she's been sent to draw our attention away. How could it not be, on today of all days?"

"She is not a weasel," Kronik said. "We have investigated her thoroughly. We have even collected samples of her gene plasm and compared them to the records of her mother and father. We then sent a man to Interchange to check on the fate of her parents. They were indeed sold to Hacheem Belloch, by which time her mother was undoubtedly pregnant." He pointed a finger across the table. "With her."

Thanda's hands made jerky motions. His mouth opened and closed though nothing came out as he looked from Morwen to Kronik. Then he sucked in a long, audible breath and said, "Give her to me. We'll get the truth out of her."

Now it was Kronik's turn to shake his head. "No, you won't. Besides, she is a registered member of this community —"

"From which she was apprehended, trying to flee!" Thanda said.

"Even so. But she is covered by the Covenant. I have jurisdiction over her, and I mean to exercise it."

Thanda's face went pale, save for two red spots that appeared on his prominent cheekbones. He told Kronik he could do something anatomically impossible with the Covenant, then said, "I'm taking her."

While Thanda had been speaking, Kronik had quietly drawn his sidearm. The other deputy in the room now drew his.

Kronik said, "There are more of us than your Protectors, and we are not unarmed farmers and townsfolk. Right now, the two of my constables you suborned have been disarmed and confined to the cells.

"Push this, and it will not go well for you. I will arrest you now and lock you away." He paused to let that sink in then added, "And you wouldn't want that, today of all days."

Silence, and the tension grew. Until Morwen broke it.

"I have a question," she said.

Thanda and Kronik both turned toward her. "Ask it," the scrutineer said.

"All I know of Interchange is what my parents and the other slaves could tell me. I know slaves can be bought out of bondage there, if the price is right."

"I don't hear a question," Thanda said.

"What I don't know," Morwen said, "is what that costs."

"Nor do I," said Kronik, "but I can send someone to find out."

Thanda was regarding Morwen with the hard look of a man who still thought he might be on the receiving end of a confidence trick. She returned his gaze as guilelessly as she could. After a long wait, Thanda said, "I might know. What kind of slaves are they?"

"A chef and a plaincook."

"Their ages?"

Morwen gave their ages, in standard years.

Thanda looked at the opposite wall. He pulled the inside corner of his mouth between his teeth as he calculated. Finally, he said, "Depending on how highly their master prizes their culinary skills, I would estimate at least 20,000 SVU for him, 10,000 for her. At the most, 40,000 and 20,000."

"So, the maximum would be 60,000 SVU," Morwen said.

"The master might also extort a bonus," Thanda speculated. "Perhaps an additional 10,000."

Morwen nodded, accepting the calculation. "So, 70,000 SVU would free my parents. And a few hundred more would transport them here and get them resettled."

"Here?" said Kronik."

"It's a livable community," she said, then glancing at Thanda, added, "by and large."

Thanda cleared his throat, or it might have been a growl. "What of it?"

Morwen indicated the bead in Kronik's hand. "That was the most prized possession of the head of a major crime family on a wealthy world in the Oikumene. It is worth a lot more than 70,000 SVU."

"But it's deeply encrypted," Kronik said. "We don't know what it is worth, or how to access the wealth."

"You don't," Morwen said, offering an apologetic smile. "But I do. And my parents believed Interchange would have a device that can read it."

"I have heard of such things before," Thanda said. "Many private space ships have such readers as part of their astrogation equipment. But without the password that unlocks it —"

"I know the password," Morwen said.

At that moment, a chime sounded from the pocket in Thanda's upper garment. He fished out a small communicator and held it to his ear. A mix of expressions crossed his face as he listened: excitement, hesitation, suspicion, hope.

He settled on determination. "Carry on," he said into the device then put it away and spoke to Kronik, "It's arriving now."

The scrutineer gestured toward Morwen. "Whatever you think she might do, she can't do it from here."

Thanda looked from one to another again, and said, "If anything goes wrong…"

"It won't be our doing," Kronik said. "There are no weasels in New Dispensation."

"I will hold you to that," Thanda said, and left.

Kronik put away his sidearm, folded his hands and regarded Morwen with quiet expectation. She said, "Today, of all days? What is that all about?"

He smiled. "You haven't worked that out? I took you for an intelligent woman."

"I know he's been building a landing pad," she began, then was struck by the obvious. "Of course. That's where all the money has gone."

"Exactly," said Kronik. He pocketed the little ball and said, "If you promise not to run away, we'll go and watch."

"I'm not going anywhere without that bead," she said.

"Just so," Kronik said. He got up and opened the door.

It began as a small, dark dot high in the west, descending as it flew toward the town. Kronik had led Morwen to the town hall's roof, where a landing stage for aircars had been part of the original design. Clerks and constables were already gathered there, watching, exchanging murmurs of conversation as those in the know informed those from whom the knowledge had been kept.

Morwen squinted and shaded her eyes. Beside her, Kronik said, "Do you know the type?"

She waited until the object had grown nearer and thus larger. "Not a commercial craft," she said. "A private space yacht." She peered again. "By those forward sponsons, I'd guess an Itinerator class, Mark III or IV."

"Very good," Kronik said. "A Mark III, used but refitted at the Fitzwen Yards on New Chilliwhack."

"That's an Oikumene world," Morwen said. "Isn't it…well, risky to buy a craft that the IPCC may have meddled with?"

"Somewhat, but Thanda will go over it very carefully. One of his Protectors has the technical background."

"Assuming," said Morwen, "that the technician is not himself a weasel."

"Unlikely," said Kronik. "And here it comes."

The yacht was black, with crimson sponsons fore and after, and a thin white strip from bow to stern. It came down from the sky in a spiral, slowing as it descended, until it barely kissed the concrete pad as it settled beside the Manse.

"Somebody knows how to fly," Morwen said.

"Lech Macrine. He's Thanda's pilot," Kronik said. He turned toward the descending staircase. "Thanda is going to be busy for a while. You and I need to talk."

Morwen looked him straight in the eye. "I won't tell what I know until we're at Interchange."

"That," said the scrutineer, "is just one of the things we need to talk about."

• • •

Much of the town had come out to see the descent of the Itinerator III and were standing in the street and on the sidewalks discussing the event when Morwen left the town hall. She saw Gisby and Terelia outside the restaurant, then noted the confusion and concern that appeared on their faces when they saw Kronik come down the steps after her, take her elbow, and hand Morwen her ditty bag. A deputy came around from the rear of the building, wheeling her bicycle that had been stored in the basement evidence room.

Morwen waved at her employers, put the bag in the basket, and mounted the bike. It was time for pre-dinner prep, so she rode the short distance to where Gisby and Terelia waited expectantly.

"It's a long story," she said, before they could ask. "I'll tell you later."

They accepted it, though they exchanged one of those freighted looks that long-married couples develop. Morwen parked the bike, carried her bag inside, and went into the kitchen. She found a knife and began to chop vegetables.

At the evening dinner service, she came out of the kitchen carrying two plates of shumkin pie to find Bod Hipple seated at the counter.

He regarded her with a sour expression.

"You told me," he said, "there was nothing between you and that Hubbley."

She took the plates to a table where a farmer and his wife showed more interest in what the mechanic had said than in the food she placed before them. Then she returned to where Bod sat.

"I know it was you," she said.

For a moment, he was abashed, then his mien again became accusatory. "Eldo Kronik asked me to keep an eye on you. When you found the bike."

She put her fists on her hips. "So this courtship has just been you playing Kronik's weasel."

His lower lip protruded. "No, but —" He caught himself and returned to safer ground. "How do you explain yourself? What's between you and Hubbley?"

"Nothing. I told you, he gave me a ride from Hambledon to the crossroads hotel."

Bod sneered. "And the experience meant so much to you that you had to chase him down like a love-sick cheechee."

The reference took Morwen aback. "What's a cheechee?"

The farmwife at the nearby table said, "It's a half-grown female shumkin." She gestured at the pie before her.

Bod rounded on her. "Do you mind?"

She gave him the facial equivalent of a shrug but did not look away.

Morwen said, "I had to leave New Dispensation. I did not want Kronik, or anyone, to know I had gone. Hubbley seemed my only recourse."

Now confusion and suspicion warred in Bod Hipple's face. "Why?" he said. "Are you a weasel after all? Kronik said —"

"If I were, do you think I would be cooking dinners and arguing with the customers?"

A bell chimed from the kitchen. Morwen reflexively turned toward the swinging door.

Bod said, "I don't understand."

"No," Morwen said, "you don't. So I'll tell you. Up until not long ago, I was someone's possession. I will not be anyone's possession, ever again. And certainly not yours."

The farm wife caught her eye and gave Morwen a firm nod. Then the bell chimed again, and she went into the kitchen.

Kronik had released her from custody. Thanda had not been pleased, but had finally accepted that Morwen would not go anywhere without the encrypted orb. Kronik had made him understand that she had spent her whole life preparing to obtain the object, and had taken great risks to escape Hacheem Belloch's estate and cross vast distances of the immensity to find it.

Besides, Thanda had other goals to pursue. Seated together in his office, the senior scrutineer had explained it to her: the proceeds of two years' production and sale of maunch extract had gone into the purchase of the Itinerator III. Now Thanda's operation would no longer be dependent on ships operating out of Hambledon spaceport.

"Smuggling is expensive," Kronik said. "Those who risk arrest and incarceration expected to be well paid for their perils. Now Thanda can retain those funds, some of which will be used to improve conditions in New Dispensation. You may have noticed that the water distribution system is antiquated. Now it can be renewed."

So Thanda and his Protectors would eliminate the cost-producing middlers. They would take their extract direct to market in the rich worlds of the Oikumene, some of whose louche denizens were willing to pay well for the pleasures of mind-freeing substances forbidden by local authorities.

The scrutineer showed a philosophic mien. "Ironically, the Horths on New Bruges have been regular customers. Now, Thanda can offer them a discounted price if they take more product."

The news had alarmed Morwen. "Will he offer them the bead?" she said.

"He cannot. I have it and he will not get it. We will take it to Interchange, discover its true value, and use some of that value to emancipate your parents."

"Why would you do that for me?"

His expression now became complex. "I will do it largely for myself. It means I do not have to torture you for the key, which, despite my having been thoroughly trained by the Deweaseling Corps, I would find unpleasant."

"I, too," said Morwen.

Kronik thought that was worth a slight smile. "Also, I exist here in a state of conflict. I still adhere to the ideas of the Society of the New Dispensation. Maunch has opened my being. Things being as they are, however—which means Thanda being the power that he is—I must make accommodations."

He shifted in his seat and looked out the window at the stone house where Protectors were loading the yacht with small crates of extract. "Thanda is a benefit to the community. My constables and I can restrain his worst inclinations, and he knows that his remit of fear and intimidation runs only so far.

"So we exist in equilibrium. I am not pleased with it, but when I find a way to live more closely within the philosophy that brought us all here, I take it."

"I see," said Morwen. She studied his hard face for a moment, and saw honesty. "Thank you."

Kronik waved away gratitude, as Dispers usually did. "Besides," he said, "I have come to approve of you. You are, in your own way, an admirable person."

The morning after the conversation between Morwen and Bod, the town heard the hum of the space yacht's drive cycling up. Many came out into the street or went to their windows to watch the vessel rise from its pad, raise its nose, and begin to climb. In not very long, it was a tiny dot in the sky, then it was gone.

Kronik had told her that it was expected to take three days, using the Jarnell intersplit, to reach Oikumene space. Then there would be a number of worlds to visit, before it turned back toward Providence. It would arrive after about ten days, its hold empty of the extract but filled with bundles of currency.

Then the matter of a trip to Interchange would be discussed and settled.

Morwen continued to work at the restaurant. She had had a conversation with Gisby and Terelia, who had at first been aggrieved at her sudden decampment. But when she explained why and what, the couple went off and spoke together.

When they came back, Gisby said, "Your intent is to free your parents then return here?"

"Yes."

"With them?"

"It was their home."

Gisby nodded then moved on to the next point. He gestured to the restaurant around them. "And this was their livelihood."

"That was long ago," said Morwen. "I believe we can work something out."

Terelia spoke then. "We would not like to lose you, dear. Even to your own kin."

"Slavery," said Morwen, "changes the way you think, the way you feel. My parents will be happy wherever they are, whatever they are doing, so long as they are doing it without a whip over them."

So, that was settled.

. . .

It was eleven days before the Itinerator returned. As it settled onto its pad, Eldo Kronik arrived at the restaurant, where the after-lunch clean-up was in progress.

"It's time," he said. "Go home and change, then meet me at the constabulary."

Morwen did so. When she came into Kronik's office, wearing her spacer's garb, he handed her her projac. "It's fully charged," he said. "Best not to make a show of it."

Morwen placed the weapon in the top of her ditty bag. "Ready to go," she said.

They boarded the scrutineer's ground car along with two of the deputies. The route took them up the switchbacks. Morwen looked at the little white house as they passed it and felt a mix of emotions. When they reached the level ground where the sprawling stone house stood, Thanda and one of his Protectors were waiting.

"That's Lech Macrine," Kronik said, "the pilot."

The scrutineers' vehicle pulled up beside the yacht's pad. Kronik, Morwen, and one of the deputies got out. Kronik sent the constabulary car and driver back down the hill.

Thanda gave the three of them a sour look. "You have us outnumbered," he said.

Kronik's reply was bland. "She is not mine. Consider her a neutral third party, with her own interests to pursue. She might even end up siding with you."

Thanda snorted his disbelief in such an outcome. "Let's get aboard."

The Itinerator had clearly had a life before it became a drug-runner's get-about, but it was well maintained and clean. There were staterooms for the quality and smaller cabins for the crew and servants. Morwen chose one of the latter, the farthest aft in the yacht's central corridor. She deposited her ditty bag on the bunk, then extracted the projac and tucked it into the waistband of her breeches, underneath the fall of her spacer's tunic. Then she set the door lock to a seven-digit combination and went forward, where she found the others gathered in the saloon.

The appointments were luxurious, although the fabric on the plush furniture showed some wear. The four men were standing on the faded red-and-gold Arakh carpet, and Macrine was telling Kronik they would need almost a full day's travel through normal space before engaging the intersplit. It would transit them instantly to a point several hours distant from the planet Sasani, which orbited a star named Aquila in the far reaches of the Beyond.

"Interchange is far out in a desert called the Da'ar-Rizm," he continued, "but we can't land there."

"Why not?" Kronik said.

"Any private spacecraft approaching the place is assumed to be an IPCC raid. We'd be targeted by a ring of ison cannons and —" the pilot wiggled the fingers of both hands in a descending motion "— reduced to a rain of glowing fragments."

He said they would land at a spaceport in Nichae on the shores of a shallow sea and board an airship that would carry them out to a desert station called Sul Arsam. "Then it's a surface vehicle that trundles out to Interchange, about an hour's ride."

Kronik addressed Thanda. "Anything more we should know?"

Thanda said, "I have acquired a reader for beads such as yours and have had it installed in the cockpit."

Kronik said, "Then we should see if it can tell us anything."

The five of them trooped to the confined space, where the reader was mounted on one of the control panels. Kronik produced the bead and placed it in a circular receptacle on the top of the device. An indicator light glowed red and a voice spoke from the reader: "Password."

The men looked at Morwen. "No," she said. She took a step back from them and let her hand find the butt of the projac that she had slipped into her breeches' waistband at the small of her back.

Kronik raised his hand in acknowledgement that nothing had changed. "We will wait until we are at Interchange," he said.

Lech Macrine said, "The fact that it fits into a device used for astrogation, and that it belonged to the head of an Oikumene crime family…" He cocked his head to indicate that the conclusion was obvious.

It was not obvious to Jerz Thanda. "What?"

"Treasure map," said Macrine, "the treasure hidden somewhere in the Beyond."

Thanda's immediate response was a snort of disbelief. Then his expression changed, and he touched the bead with a finger. He looked at Morwen.

"When we get to Interchange," she said. "That's what we agreed."

Thanda continued to hold her gaze. She watched him weigh up his options. Finally, he said, "As agreed."

Kronik recovered the bead and put it in his pocket.

They returned to the saloon. Morwen was about to return to her cabin when she remembered something her parents had told her. "At Interchange, there are winged insects in the desert. Flesh-eaters. The guards had protection. They found the antics of the slaves amusing."

Kronik looked at Thanda. "You've been to Interchange, haven't you?"

The man's shrug was a confession.

"And you have something to keep the bugs away?"

Thanda admitted that he had laid in a couple of ultrasonic inhibitors. "Turned to maximum, they will keep the creatures away from all of us."

"That is good," said Kronik. "I would be devastated if, while aiming my projac at some carnivorous insect, I was to accidentally beam a hole through some part of your person." He waved a hand in conjecture. "Perhaps some part you are particularly fond of."

As ship's time wore on to evening, it was discovered that none of Morwen's fellow travelers were adept in the culinary arts. She volunteered to prepare supper. Whatever she made would taste better and it would remove the possibility that Thanda, experienced in the use of psychoactive chemicals, might adulterate her food with some substance to weaken her will and enable him to command her to divulge the password. The galley was well equipped — the previous owner had employed a chef — and the larder was stocked with pre-packaged foods and some basic materials.

She baked some rolls and made a stew out of freeze-dried meat and vegetables. The spice rack contained a few half-full vials of interesting flavors, so she was able to improve what would otherwise have been a bland meal. She brewed up a pot of black tea and served scones for "afters."

Thanda and his man ate without comment then withdrew. Kronik sent his deputy to keep an eye on them then helped Morwen clear the table and arrange the dishes in the cleanser.

She stood back and watched him load the last few plates and cutlery. "You don't strike me as the kind of man who is comfortable with Thanda's kind," she said.

He did not turn to her. "Comfortable?" His head moved from side to side in a gesture of equivocation. "I'm not 'comfortable.' But there are practicalities to consider."

"Such as?"

He turned to her and itemized his points on his fingers. "He is the legitimate successor to the Prophet. Or at least a good portion of our population have accepted him as such.

"He is not a capricious tyrant. If he is left alone to do as he does, he leaves us alone to do as we do.

"Under the Covenant we negotiated after he expanded maunch production, he has contributed substantially to the common purse, so that our people are not taxed beyond their means to provide necessities like power, water, getting the roads fixed."

He touched the last finger. "Whereas ridding ourselves of him and his Protectors would get some of us killed."

Morwen nodded. "Hacheem Belloch offers similar benefits to the people he lurks amongst. Oddly enough, the prosperity he provides is not as much now as it once was, while his appetite for opulence has increased."

Kronik nodded in return. "It is an old pattern. I watch to see how it evolves, and will make my choices accordingly."

They slept behind closed doors. In what they called the morning, Thanda activated the intersplit and they felt the skin-shivering moment of strangeness as the ship's drive rearranged the universe to their benefit. Soon after, they heard the drive sigh its way into quietude as they transited back into normal space. The yellow star Aquila was now centered in the saloon's forward viewing screen, pea-sized but enlarging with each passing moment.

They touched down at the Nichae spaceport, sealed the yacht's hatches, and passed through the terminal to where the airship left every hour. It was mid-day on this part of Sasani when they boarded, mid-afternoon when the aircraft descended to its short tethering mast outside a huddle of flat-roofed structures of mudbrick and white stone that the ship's operator announced as Sul Arsam. A battered, long-bodied vehicle resting on four fat tires awaited them some distance away, its driver leaning against the dusty side with an expectant grin on his face.

Thanda activated his sonic repellent and Macrine did likewise. They stepped down from the airship's gondola and paused so Morwen and the two scrutineers could close in upon them, then they marched as a tight-packed quintet toward the disreputable old bus.

The other passengers, unwarned, found themselves under assault from a cloud of black insects that swept up from burrows in the ground and attacked any uncovered flesh, each biting off a minuscule but painful mouthful and flying away to deliver it to their grubs. The victims screamed and cursed and flailed their hands about their faces and necks, as they ran stumbling across the distance to the bus. Morwen and the Dispers marched stolidly on until they passed the grinning driver and boarded the vehicle.

The ride out to Interchange was only slightly less comfortable than the dash to escape the biters. The bus's suspension was a faint memory and they drove not on any semblance of a road but over the naked desert ground, which was rutted and pitted from the effects of seasonal floods brought on by infrequent, though torrential, rains. The driver's seat was cushioned, while the passengers sat on bare metal.

Their first sight of Interchange was the tumble of crumbling ocher sandstone rising above the desert's flat horizon, with a grove of feather-leafed trees at its crown. As they grew nearer, Morwen could make out the low-built concrete structures straggling along the base of the great reddish mound. They were gray and utilitarian-looking, and she imagined how they must have appeared to her parents as the slave carrier rumbled toward them.

The bus slowed and entered a walled space, then stopped on a paved apron. Grinning again, the driver opened the door. Another swarm of flesh-biters rose up as the passengers followed a series of yellow arrows across the tarmac to the nondescript door that bore a sign: *Reception.*

Inside, the new arrivals were confronted by a counter behind which a diminutive clerk whose skullcap bore the clasped-hands symbol of Interchange made entries in a ledger. He disdained to notice their presence. A sign instructed them: *Take a seat and wait.*

Most of the people from the bus shuffled across the tiled floor and sat. Thanda stared at the functionary for a long moment, then advanced to the barrier. The clerk ignored him. Thanda waited a little longer, then rapped his knuckles on the counter top.

The small man paused in his notations, then went back to work.

Thanda spoke quietly. "You are probably used to people who creep in here, intimidated by the circumstances under which they must pay the ransom that frees their loved ones from bondage."

The clerk did not look Thanda's way, but Morwen saw that he now had the little man's attention. She also saw him glance toward a button nearby on the counter top.

"I am not such a person," Thanda said. "But I am the sort of person who never forgets an insult, no matter how slight. Moreover, I am of the kind who can wait quite a long time to repay the affront, and during that period I can be most inventive in deciding exactly what punishment is merited."

The clerk now ignored the button. He put down his stylus and showed Thanda an attentive face. "How may I help you, Ser...?"

"My name is of no moment. You may help me by providing information about this facility."

"At your service, Ser."

Thanda leaned on the counter. "Interchange holds funds until they can be disbursed as kidnap-ransom and the hostages released, yes?"

The clerk said that the correct terminology was "fees" for the "rescission" of "guests." How the guests came to be housed at the facility was beyond Interchange's purview.

"I do not care what the terminology is," Thanda said. "Is my assumption correct?"

"It is."

"Therefore, you are a kind of bank."

The functionary's first instinct appeared to be an inclination to argue, but a glance at Thanda's face vitiated whatever energy the impulse grew out of.

"Kind of, I suppose."

"Good," said Thanda. "We are making progress."

Thanda indicated his party ranged behind him. "We wish to open an account and deposit funds into it. We then wish to use some of those funds to purchase the liberty of some persons who were sold out of here more than twenty standard years ago."

The clerk looked apologetic. "That is not our normal business. Once guests' fees have been paid, they are discharged and no longer our concern."

"Regard my degree of patience," Thanda said, "as I expand your concept of where your 'concern' lies. You are accustomed to charging management fees for certain services, correct?"

"Correct."

"One such service could be to consult your records as to the 'rescission' of the fees for the two persons in question?"

"Yes."

"Which would identify the name and contact information of the party who paid those fees?"

The clerk visibly swallowed. "That information would be kept in confidence."

"Only appropriate," said Thanda. "But there would be nothing preventing Interchange from contacting that person and making an offer on behalf of a third party to bring the persons in question here for a substantial fee, would there?"

The little man thought about it. "Unconventional," he said after a while, "but conceivable. Of course, we would have to charge a commission."

"Of what percentage?"

The brow beneath the clasped hands symbol furrowed. "I would have to consult my manager."

"Make an estimate," said Thanda. "I will not hold you to it."

The clerk's narrow shoulders rose and fell. "Twelve and a half percent?" he guessed. "Fifteen, even?"

"That would not be insurmountable. Pray consult your superior."

The man went through a door at the rear wall, closing it after him.

One of the other passengers on the bus spoke up from the row of chairs. "Some of us have important business to transact."

Another said, "Loved ones to ransom."

Thanda turned and met the gaze of each speaker in turn, until each subsided. He turned back to the counter as the clerk reentered.

"My manager says we will allow funds to be deposited pending a rescission of fees. No interest will be paid. And we will collect a fifteen percent commission on the transaction."

"Agreed," said Thanda. "Draw up a document."

"I have already done so," said the clerk, producing a piece of paper with some hint of a flourish.

Thanda scanned the document, then turned to Morwen. "Is this satisfactory to you?"

She came and read. It was a simple rendition of the terms she had heard discussed. "It is."

There were spaces for signatures. She applied hers and Thanda wrote his own. The clerk took a stamp from a drawer and put Interchange's seal on the document.

He said, "You may now deposit the funds."

Thanda turned to Morwen with an expression that said it was her turn to act. She held out her hand. Kronik stepped forward and placed the bead in it. She asked the clerk for a reading device and he brought one from a back shelf. She placed the bead in the receptacle and pressed the activating stud. The reader hummed for a moment then its voice said, "Password."

Morwen maintained an outward calm, but this was the moment where conjecture met reality. In Purpuram Gratz's household, her mother had often been required to bring refreshments to his study. Twice, she had arrived with a tray of liqueurs and essences while he had been seated with his back to the door, the bead in his hand, softly mouthing an unusual word.

Morwen and her parents had discussed the matter and had come to the conclusion that the odd string of syllables was the code that unlocked the encryption. But they had never been able to test the theory; activating the bead required a device that could read it. No such device existed in Mount Pleasant. Then the Demon Princes came.

So, the password had long been an article of faith to Morwen and her parents. And now that faith would be tested. She bent to bring her mouth close to the reader, cupped her hands around its sound receptor, and whispered the string of nonsense syllables she had known since childhood, "Noxxifloxxibohintafedang."

The machine clicked twice and a screen appeared in the air above it. The screen filled from top to bottom with a series of letters and numbers. The clerk and the people from New Dispensation studied the display.

The clerk was the first to speak. "That is not a financial document."

"No," said Thanda, his face darkening, "it isn't."

Lech Macrine closed in and studied the figures. "It's a location. In space. Somewhere far down the Beyond."

The clerk made a sound of irritation. "You have wasted my time." He picked up the piece of paper in a theatrical gesture, and showed the intent of tearing it in two.

Thanda reached for it and the man let it go. "We will be back," he said. "The same arrangement will stand."

The clerk made a little noise that expressed his doubt in the prediction. Meanwhile Thanda scooped the bead out of the reader, took Morwen by the arm, and propelled her toward the door. Kronik and the other two followed.

"You made a fool of me," Thanda said as he pushed Morwen toward where the bus stood, its driver visible through the side window eating his lunch. The insects rose up then swirled away from the ultrasonics.

"No," said Morwen. She yanked her arm free of his grip, her mind working furiously. "I was wrong about what the encryption concealed. But I was not wrong about its value."

They had reached the bus. "Get aboard," Thanda said.

Morwen climbed in, followed by the scrutineers and the Protector. Thanda boarded last. He spoke to the driver. "We are going to talk among ourselves. You would do well not to listen."

To emphasize his point, he opened the front of his upper garment to show the butt of a projac.

The five went to the back of the vehicle and Kronik spoke first. "What was that all about?"

Thanda was about to speak but Morwen cut him off. "It was an astrogation 'address,' far down the galactic arm, almost to the Great Dark. A world."

Kronik said, "We should get back to the ship and look it up in the Star Record."

Macrine signaled a negative. "We won't find it."

Thanda caught on. "Yes, you don't encrypt an address that's available for anyone to look up."

"A hidden world," Kronik said.

Morwen had been thinking. "Some locator found it, but didn't come back and offer it for auction. Maybe he or she was tightly contracted to a single investor, or maybe the first to hear of the discovery took steps to ensure no one else would ever have that knowledge.

"Either way, there are people who would pay a fortune to own a world nobody else knows exists."

Thanda smiled. "And only we know where it is."

Kronik matched his expression. "We need to go there, make sure we know what we are selling."

Back in the Itinerator III, Thanda led the way to the cockpit, where the bead reader sat atop the yacht's astrogation system. He placed the orb in the receptacle. "Speak the password," he ordered Morwen.

"Not until you all step out."

She saw anger flare in Thanda's pale face, then saw it suppressed. He waved all of them out of the small space and closed the door. Morwen whispered the string of nonsense and saw the screen fill with characters that represented complex triple vectors. She transferred the image to the astrogation pick-up, then put the bead back in her pocket.

"Come in," she called. When the door opened, she pressed the stud that told the astrogation system to prepare to engage with the drive. A series of readouts came to life and a sign flashed: *Ready to engage.*

Macrine stepped forward and took a look at the readouts. "We've got a ways to go," he said. "I recommend we return to normal space here —" he touched one of the displays that was slowly ticking off points on a necklace of dots "— and go the rest of the way quiet and careful."

"Sensible," said Kronik. "We don't know what might be waiting for us."

"Let's go," Thanda said. There were no formalities involved in leaving Sasani. The yacht lifted off, exited the atmosphere and oriented itself downward relative to the galactic arm. They traveled at maximum speed long enough to leave Aquila's system, then engaged the Jarnell intersplit.

The usual strangeness fell upon them for a timeless period, then the ship's systems brought them back to the phenomenal universe. They gathered in the forward saloon and studied the wide screen's display of what lay before them: a great swathe of blackness, unlit by stars.

"A gas cloud," said Morwen. "A big one."

"Big enough to hide a star and its planets?" said Thanda.

"Yes," said his pilot. "We should go in slow."

They tuned the yacht's forward sensors to maximum and entered the cloud at a modest speed. The hiss of thinly disseminated hydrogen molecules streaming against the hull became a constant background to their conversation. After a while, the conversation lapsed completely.

Until Macrine, studying the readouts, said, "Change coming."

They gathered before the screen again. The hiss faded then stopped as the yacht emerged from the gas. Deep in the immense cloud, they had come upon a huge rift. In the open space they saw a small white star circled by a number of planets, including a vast sphere of condensed gas and a few made of rock and ice. The second from the star, when they viewed it through the macroscope, showed the presence of air and water and rudimentary vegetation.

It was smaller than most viable worlds, aged and worn down by time. There was a single continent occupying much of the northern hemisphere, mostly flat and bounded on all sides by tideless gray seas that dully reflected the sun's skimpy light.

The yacht shed speed and settled into a close orbit. The macroscope showed lichens and mosses, nothing that could be described as a tree or even a shrub. The land fauna were creeping things, none larger than a man's hand, though there may have been more substantial creatures in the depths of the ocean. The air was breathable though the white dwarf did not warm it much.

Where the single continent's southern edge met the sea was the only noticeable geographic feature: a high eminence, sheer-sided, with a small, flat space at its peak. Thanda told Macrine to land the yacht there.

They stepped out into cold, damp air. The white star, a high dot shining through gray overcast, shed light but little warmth. They could smell the reek of rotting vegetation washed up on the shore below. The world also had its own, sour smell, as if the atmosphere was tinged with corrosive acid.

"A forlorn place," Kronik said. "No one's idea of a vacation paradise."

"But if you wanted a place to be undisturbed…" Thanda said.

Morwen shivered, and not just from the damp chill. "Probably what Gratz wanted it for." She didn't want to think about what use its eventual purchaser might make of this world. Her goal was to free her parents. If, afterward, she had to live with guilt, so be it.

"Let's get some images," she said. "The potential buyers will want to see what they're bidding for."

"An auction?" said Kronik.

"Good idea," said Thanda, "but with a select invitation list."

Chapter Five

For Morwen, it was a long journey back to Providence, her lifelong plan to rescue her parents having crashed onto the reef of a false assumption that the encrypted bead contained vast wealth. She spent most of her time in her small cabin, replaying the events in the reception room at Interchange, where all her hopes had been brought to nothing.

A part of her told her that there was still an avenue toward her goal, but the small gleam at the end of that route was continually overshadowed by the darkness that surrounded her and impinged on her sense of being a woman of competence.

The men stopped asking her to prepare meals and simply reheated what was in the stores. Kronik and Thanda spoke often over the refectory table or in the saloon, proposing the mechanisms of the planned auction, the potential invitees, the safe and secure means to approach them without the event being taken for an IPCC operation meant to lure them into a trap.

Thanda had some reputation in the law-evading circles of the Beyond, having connected with criminal organizations on several planets. He also had contacts among the halfworlds of the Oikumene. He mentioned names, some of which were unknown to Kronik, others known widely.

His problem, however, was that he primarily dealt with mid-level gang chiefs and operators of distribution networks for his psychedelic product. The counsels of the master criminals were not open to him. It would take time and sustained effort to make his way safely up the ladder to reach the people who would have the wealth and the appetite to own a secret, hidden world.

Kronik said, "What about the five who turned New Dispensation into a ghost town? The so-called Demon Princes?"

Thanda shrugged. "Some of them have not been heard of in a while. That probably means they are planning fresh outrages. But there is a rumor that some force is at play to their detriment." He gave Kronik a meaningful look. "To their final detriment, if you take my meaning."

Kronik hovered somewhere between skepticism and being impressed. "That would be some force," he said. "Each of them is high on the IPCC's shoot-on-sight list."

Thanda moved his lips in a dismissive moue. "It is only a rumor, perhaps arising out of the law-abiding folk's desire to see extravagant evil brought to heel."

"A hope not often realized," Kronik said.

The conversation moved on to more productive concerns.

When Providence showed as a blue and white dot in the forward screen, Kronik knocked on the door of Morwen's cabin. Listless, she told him to come in.

He closed the door behind him and said, "You know more about space ships than I do. Isn't there some system that tells where a ship has been?"

She nodded. "There's a monitor. It records everything on a wire filament, and creates a metal coding strip that encrypts the information." Her eyes widened as she realized the implications of what she was saying.

"Exactly," said Kronik. "We need that strip. Do you know how to access it?"

"I've never done it, but I know where it ought to be."

They went forward to the part of the ship where the controls were. It was called by an ancient term — "the cockpit" — whose derivation was lost in the shadows of the far past so that no one today knew the origin. Morwen had heard a couple of attempts to explain the etymology, but dismissed both of them as ridiculous.

Thanda and Macrine were in the refectory, drinking punge, their heads together, conversing in low tones. Kronik and Morwen passed the doorway without a word. The deputy scrutineer was at the entrance to the cockpit, where Kronik had stationed him. He stood aside as Morwen went into the small chamber.

Thanda and his pilot came up the corridor. Kronik and the deputy blocked their way. Meanwhile, Morwen went to the small hatch, clearly marked, behind which lay the controls for the monitor. She flipped it open, then unlatched a smaller covering to reveal a spool of shining metal filament fixed in its own compartment. It took two snaps to free the coding strip from its housing. She turned to see the four men struggling in the doorway.

The cockpit had its own hatch to space. She opened the in-ship side, threw the strip of metal into the opening, closed it and pressed the stud that opened the far side of the airlock. The air gasped out into space as a mist of sparkling ice crystals, the coding strip going with it.

The struggle in the doorway ended.

Kronik said, "So, that's that."

Thanda's expression was sour, but there was nothing to be done.

Returned to New Dispensation, Morwen went back to work at the restaurant, though now she was again an object of curiosity, as she had been upon her first arrival. But both Kronik and Thanda, each in his own way, had spread the word that, whatever they were up to, it was not to be bruited about. Thanda came to the Firstday meet-up and addressed the congregation.

"The addition of a space yacht to our community is liable to draw renewed attention from the IPCC," he told them. "As always, be mindful of strangers. Report any suspicions to the constabulary. But the surest way to prevent them hearing what we don't want them to hear, is to say nothing to each other.

"And be assured that everything said in New Dispensation makes its way to my hearing."

Bod Hipple had stopped coming to the restaurant for lunch. But not long after Morwen returned from Interchange, Tosh Hubbley parked his carryall outside and came through the door. He sat at the counter and ordered punge and pie.

"I was concerned for you," he told Morwen, "worried you might be taken for a weasel."

"You might have the same fear for yourself," she told him, lowering her voice. "The new thing happens up there —" she cocked her head toward the mountain "— and suddenly you're changing your habits. Such things are noticed."

"I have been well vetted by the Deweaseling Corps," he said. "My ancestry is thoroughly documented. My people were farmers near Worstead. That's a village two days walk from Hambledon. The original Hubbleys arrived on the second colony ship, generations ago. My parents sold the farm to cousins, put all their goods in a horse-drawn wagon, and moved to Hambledon to open a business. I was born in the wagon on the way. If I am a weasel, I must have been recruited in the womb."

"Still, we are seeing members of the Deweaseling Corps Jerz Thanda has called to town. They are serious. And ruthless."

Hubbley half-laughed. "I'll be careful. Besides now that you have assuaged my fears, I can return to my harmless old habits."

The omnibus arrived from Hambledon. From the café window, Morwen saw it stop then rumble on, leaving Dedana Llanko on the pavement, two filled shopping bags in her hands. Morwen had been waiting for the chance to talk with the old woman and now she told Terelia she would be right back and hurried across Broadway to catch the hotel owner before she finished her laborious climb up the front steps.

Coming up behind Llanko, she took one of the bags from her. The woman turned in alarm but Morwen assured her she was only looking to help.

Llanko's brows formed their habitual vee. "Why?"

"Because you're one of the original colonists. You knew my parents when they had the café."

The woman pushed through the hotel's front door, deposited her bag on the old carpet within, and turned as Morwen followed her. "So?" she said.

"So you can tell me about them. About the raid."

"No, I can't. I wasn't here." She gestured toward the bags. "Then as now, we got toiletries from Hambledon." She sighed. "I was away, getting soaps and depilatories. The omnibus was coming up from Brumble's Corners when we saw the ships rising into the sky.

"When we got to town, we saw the bodies in the streets, the dead constables. I came in, shouting for Watto, my husband. There was no answer. They'd taken him."

Her face collapsed.

"I'm sorry," Morwen said. "I shouldn't have —"

Dedana Llanko was lost in the past now. "Nobody who was in town survived that day. I went into the street. I thought I should move the bodies. It was unseemly to leave them lying there, all burned and chopped. But it was too much. The omnibus driver and the other passengers wouldn't help me. They just wanted to get away.

"Then old Rolf Gersen came up from the river, with his grandson Kirth in their carryall. They'd taken a barge full of produce to Hambledon and had just got back. Together, we buried the dead. It was an awful thing. Kirth's parents had been killed.

"Soon after, the Gersens left everything behind. That old man was vowing revenge on the Demon Princes." She snorted. "What chance would they have, a graybeard and a stripling? Still, they went to Hambledon and got on a space ship, supposedly bound for Earth, whence we had come. I don't know what happened to them."

"I'm sorry," Morwen said again. "I just wanted to know what my parents were like before…"

The old woman shrugged. "What does it matter? We are what we are now, and what we were…" She opened her hands as if letting a bird fly away. "It's all gone. Forever."

The Deweaseling Corps operatives flooded into town, resolved to ensure the proposed auction was not an IPCC plot. They stood out from the Dispers and Protectors. They wore the costumes common on their various home worlds: tailcoats of dark fabric, tight in the shoulders but belled-out at the hips over knee-breeches and figured stockings; wide pantaloons of silken cloth below shirts with billowy sleeves under embroidered vests; close-fitting tunics over twill trousers, baggy at the knee but pegged at the ankle; flowing robes and tall headdresses.

They had first moved in at the hotel, but at Thanda's invitation rehoused themselves at the stone Manse. They spent a great deal of time at the town hall sifting through birth and residence records, and intercepted the few outsiders that came through New Dispensation, including Tosh Hubbley and the omnibus driver.

They were stern and thorough, and the possibility of sudden and conclusive violence was implied in their every word and gesture.

One day, at lunch, as Morwen was carrying four plates of her egg-and-cheese pie from the kitchen to a huddle of farmers at the window table, she realized that the subject of their conversation was Bod Hipple. She lingered after placing the food on the table and caught the gist of what they were saying.

She leaned in and said, "Did you say he's closed the repair shop?"

The men looked up and one of them said, "For good, they say."

Another said, "We're going to have to find a new mechanic."

Morwen said, "Is he leaving town?"

No, she was told. Hipple had gone "up the hill," the local term that referred to Jerz Thanda's Manse. Seeing that the reference had swept past Morwen, the farmer informed her that Bod Hipple had joined the Protectors.

"Now that Thanda's got a space ship," the man continued, "he needs someone to maintain its systems. Bod volunteered."

"You'll see him at meet-up," another put in, "black boots and projac and all."

"They shouldn't come to meet-up with projacs," a third man said. "Not right, that."

The others looked at him. "You be the one to tell them so," one of them said.

The man who had told Morwen about Hipple said, "Just make your will first and leave me that piece of pasture in the bend of the river."

Morwen was not happy to think of her former suitor in his new guise. She hadn't seen him much since he'd had her arrested, but now when their paths crossed he refused to acknowledge her. Terelia had mentioned that she had heard people mocking him behind his back.

Some of that had inevitably come down to his outsized ears. When she left the four farmers, she saw in the mirror behind the counter that their eyes followed her, then their heads moved closer together as they lowered their voices.

A day arrived when one of the Protectors came to the restaurant, charged with escorting Morwen to an interview with the Deweaseling Corps. She was driven up to the Manse in a ground car, the driver unspeaking. As they arrived, she saw the Itinerator on its pad. A service hatch was open, a man in stained coveralls halfway into the cavity. At the sound of the vehicle's arrival, he pulled himself free and watched her exit the car.

It was Bod Hipple. His face had taken on the hardness of the other Protectors. She raised a hand to wave to him, but he did not wait for her to complete the gesture. He picked up an instrument from a toolbox and returned to whatever he was doing inside the space yacht.

Her interview was with a heavy-set, bald-headed man who affected the green corduroy jacket, trousers, and five-button vest of a middle-ranked corsair of Mardey's World. Hacheem Belloch had dealt with such people. She had seen them visit the estate outside Boregore and knew she was now confronted by someone as hard-hearted as any denizen of the Beyond.

He questioned her while leafing through a file she recognized as the one Eldo Kronik had assembled.

The interrogator particularly wanted to examine her tattoo. After studying it for almost a minute, he said, "You were not manumitted by Hacheem Belloch."

It was not a question, but Morwen confirmed it. "It has been more than a year."

The man shrugged and said, "That is the convention. It may not have much sway with Hacheem Belloch." He fixed her with a direct stare. "What are your feelings about him?"

"I would gladly see him dead," she answered.

"At your own hand?"

She shrugged. "Unlikely. I am not particularly adept with weapons and he is always well guarded. Besides, it would not serve my goal, which is to free my parents. And myself."

The deweaseler studied her. "And if he were to be one of those invited to the auction?"

The question took Morwen by surprise. "Is he?"

"The list is still being discussed. But he has the wealth and likely the inclination."

A frisson of fear passed through Morwen, but she suppressed it. "I lived all my life under his rule. He was a constant factor, like gravity, like the weather. He did not steal my parents. Others did that. He only bought them and did not mistreat them. Nor me, for that matter."

She did not mention what she had seen done to other slaves at Belloch's orders.

"What if one of those who stole your parents was to attend?"

It was an issue Morwen had never considered. "The Demon Princes? I honestly don't know," she said after a long pause. "I would have to think about it."

"Would you cooperate with an IPCC weasel against such a man?"

That brought an automatic negative response from Morwen. "I have lived all my life in the Beyond," she said. "I know what happens to those who cooperate with the IPCC."

She was still being studied, evaluated. "Would you not wish to take revenge?" the deweaseler said.

Morwen looked inside herself and found the truth. "That would be for someone else to do. Slaves soon find such ambitions are beyond them. Futility sinks into the soul. My concern is for my parents."

The man continued to regard her for several heartbeats. Then he closed the file and said, "You can go."

She was not offered a ride down to the town. She walked it, conscious for the first several steps that Bod Hipple was watching her go. Halfway down, she stopped at her house. The projac was in a locked box in her bedroom. She found the key, retrieved the weapon, and tucked it in the waistband of her skirt, buttoning her cardigan over it.

Days passed. Morwen walked to the Firstday meet-up with Gisby and Terelia. Gisby was going to indulge in the sacrament today. As he went up to sit on the stage, Terelia suggested Morwen should try the experience.

Morwen was almost tempted, but she said, "Not yet. Perhaps when

I have completed my life's mission in this world, I will be ready to visit the ineffable realm."

The answer satisfied her employers. "All things in their own time," the woman said. "The sacrament teaches you that."

"So does life," Morwen said.

The service was about to start. Morwen looked around and saw Bod Hipple standing against the wall at the rear of the hall. He was not looking at her, but she had a strong impression he had been, just before her eyes found him.

She adjusted the projac under her wool jacket. Probably, it would not be needed. But if it was? She wondered if she had whatever it took to use the weapon on another human being. Perhaps it was time for her to imagine scenarios where the necessity would arise, and try to determine what she would do.

A list of invitees to the auction was decided. Next came the question of where to hold the bidding. After a short discussion between Thanda and Kronik, with an energetic input from Bao Ip, the deweaseler who had interrogated Morwen, it was decided that the only safe place to gather so many persons of interest to the IPCC was Interchange. The deweaseler was dispatched in the ship that had brought him and his colleagues to make the arrangements.

Morwen went to see Kronik after the meeting. She told him that Ip had thought Hacheem Belloch might be one of the bidders.

"He will be, if he accepts the invitation," the scrutineer said. "Maybe I should have that projac back."

"I told Ip I am no danger to Belloch. All I want is my parents free and with me." She waited while he said nothing, then added, "Besides, there is the matter of Bod Hipple."

"Ah, yes," said Kronik, "the jilted lover."

"It's not amusing," Morwen said. "And we were never lovers."

"Gossip says different," Kronik said, "although the origin of that gossip may have been…" He moved one hand, palm up, in a small circle.

Morwen finished the thought for him. "Bod Hipple. Telling everyone I was to be his intended."

Kronik gave her his usual half-smile. "Keep the projac," he said. "You may need it on Interchange."

The waiting was hard. Kronik kept her current on the delivery of the invitations, all handled through Interchange. Thanda had visited there several times, in between shipments of maunch extract to his distribution network, which was expanding now that he had his own space ship.

Belloch was one of those who were invited to bid. So was Begby Horth, who would have possessed the encrypted key decades ago, if the Morwens had not stolen it during the assault on Gratz's manor. Apparently, Kronik said, he bore no ill will and was thinking about accepting, if business affairs permitted.

"Though it is risky to take the word of a senior criminal when his vanity has been touched," the scroot told Morwen. "Still, Horth seems the cold and calculating type, not given to acting out of fits of emotion."

Kronik had taken to eating his lunch at the restaurant, saying he preferred her cooking to Gisby's. He often engaged Morwen in conversation, saying that he found her company more congenial than his colleagues at the constabulary.

"Police tend not to be interesting conversationalists," he said.

"Will it be much longer?" Morwen asked him.

"I could not say. Thanda has invited ten, telling them that only the first seven 'positive responders' will be accepted. They also have to agree to the terms, which some of them found difficult."

The terms were these: each bidder would come to New Dispensation. Each would bring no more than two retainers. Each would bring a bank draft, of a value up to that which the bidder expected to be his limit. Weapons would be stored in a secure container on the Itinerator III, which would carry them all to the world that was for sale.

They would orbit for a comprehensive view, then land for a closer inspection. The yacht would then take them to Sasani, the ship's coding strip removed from the monitor and jettisoned en route. Interchange had agreed to forgo the airship voyage and the trip across the desert on the rattling old bus. A capacious air car, under the control of Interchange staff, would collect them at the spaceport and carry them directly to the auction.

The auction would take place. The highest bidder would pay his bank draft into Interchange's fiduciary system. The facility's fifteen percent commission would be deducted, as well as 100,000 svu dedicated to the rescission of Chaffe and Elva Sabine. It was possible that Hacheem Belloch would have the pair of slaves already brought to the scene, the manumission documents for them and for Morwen Sabine already in hand.

"What if he reneges?" Morwen said.

"He has to give his word to the other bidders. They would take it as an affront to their self-esteem if he failed to honor his commitment." Kronik smiled his half-smile. "Their kind are remarkably conscious of their dignity."

"If they're like Belloch," said Morwen, "they are that, indeed."

"It all ought to go smoothly," Kronik said, over his mug of punge, "so long as everything is agreed to in advance. Settling the details is what is taking the time."

"It's hard for me," Morwen said, "the waiting."

The scrutineer confirmed that that was to be expected. "You worked all your life toward a plan and a goal. You took risks, put yourself in grave peril. Then, at the moment it all should have come right…it didn't. You found yourself in a new situation, with new players and new factors beyond your control, not to mention significant delays.

"You would have to be a heroine from a tale of derring-do not to be set back by your circumstances."

"Yes," said Morwen. She sighed then straightened her shoulders. "But I shall bear up. There is nothing else to do."

Kronik put down his mug. "If I may make a suggestion…"

Morwen gestured with both hands that she was receptive to recommendations.

Kronik said, "On the next Firstday, go to meet-up and take the sacrament. It is a good way to change the channels along which the thoughts flow. You can see yourself and your situation from a new perspective."

"A better one?"

"Not likely a worse."

She said she would think about it. Then the chime sounded from the kitchen and she went back to her work.

• • •

Terelia had advised her: "Wear something warm, but something you can take off if you get too hot. The maunch can do strange things to your body temperature."

"It gives you chills and fever?" Morwen said. "That doesn't sound —"

"Your temperature doesn't really change," the woman said. "Just the way you feel. And eat a good breakfast, for your blood sugar."

Thus, well fed and carrying a folded woolen poncho that had lain in a bureau drawer protected from insects by small, odd-smelling white spheres, Morwen arrived at the meet-up a little earlier than usual. A motherly woman took her in hand, asked her formally if she was prepared to "see what there is to see," and escorted her to the row of chairs on the stage.

Three others were to take the sacrament today: an old man with a wattled neck and the reddened hands of an outdoor worker; a young woman in a blue skirt and white blouse, with a knitted shawl about her shoulders; and a young fellow who looked to be just out of his adolescence. This last was apparently about to take the sacrament for the first time. His right leg bounced rapidly up and down as he sat in his chair, the heel beating a soft tattoo on the boards.

The motherly woman came and put a hand on his shoulder and spoke softly into his ear. The bouncing stopped and he began to take slow, regular breaths in and out. The woman then came to Morwen.

"They say it is your first opening?" she said.

Morwen swallowed. "Yes."

The woman gave her a reassuring smile and rested a plump, warm hand on Morwen's shoulder. "I will be here to guide you if you need it. There is nothing to fear. Remember, everything you experience is just a part of you. It can do you no harm."

Morwen shivered a little. The hand patted her and somehow the pressure took away some of her nervousness.

"There, you see," said the guide. "Better already."

The congregation had no leader. A man Morwen had seen often among the gathered Dispers, and occasionally at the restaurant, came up onto the stage carrying a large paper bag. He went along the row of celebrants, reaching into the sack. In front of each of the seated four he brought out a small handful of plant-stuff, which he rolled between his hands, compressing it into a tight ball. Each celebrant held out a hand and received the sacrament into his or her palm.

Morwen looked at what she had been given: a green orb of stalks and leaves. It reminded her of the encrypted bead, though it was light as air. It had a mild scent, part citrus and part something all of its own, but not unpleasant. She looked down the row of Dispers and saw each take and release a long breath, then pop the maunch into their mouths and begin to chew.

Morwen did the same. The stuff was crisp and the initial taste was somewhat like a cross between sage and mint. Copying the others, she began to chew slowly and methodically, feeling the mixed tastes suddenly blossom then subside as the maunch became a paste and her taste buds grew used to its savor.

She was chewing and thinking how the flavor might be good in a sausage when she noticed that the room had become brighter, as if curtains had been drawn back from the windows. But there were no curtains in the meeting house. Terelia had told her her pupils would expand to let in more light, but she hadn't said that everything in sight would appear to have developed sharper edges, marking one thing from another — one person from another — with distinct separateness.

Morwen was glancing around, testing this new perception when she became aware of a rush of warm energy from her lower spine up to the back of her skull. The sensation caused her to inhale, which drew the scents of maunch into her lungs and seemed to fill her entire chest with a delightful feeling of buoyancy. She felt as if she could float up to the ceiling.

I like this, she thought. *I would like to feel like this much more often.*

She continued to chew, feeling the paste like a velvet pad on her tongue. She closed her eyes to concentrate on its texture and now her mind began to fill with images. They were memories, she realized, including many from her early childhood that she had long since for-gotten. She saw her mother as a young woman, her father as a younger man, both of them gigantic — as they had seemed to Morwen as a toddler.

Most of all, she experienced their unleavened love for her. That brought a tear to her eye but then a voice spoke within her conscious-ness: *the love is never lost; it lies within you, and will be there whenever you call upon it.*

She recognized the voice as her own, inner narrator, and she was struck by its absolute aura of confidence, its assurance that all would be well. She opened her eyes and saw the congregation, the room, the windows with sunlight pouring in. It was all beautiful. It was all as it should be and would always be.

She swallowed the last of the dissolving maunch paste. The moth-erly woman came and looked into her eyes. She smiled and said, "If you wish to speak, speak."

Morwen took another breath, her lungs filling with quiet glory. She looked out over the congregation, and said, clearly, "All shall be well."

She saw Eldo Kronik in the middle of the crowd, watching her. He was smiling his half-smile and nodding. The thought came to her: *He's beautiful.*

The full effect faded quickly, but Morwen was left with a profound sense of well-being, though the engrossing images and insights dimin-ished along with the last sensations brought by the drug. Wearing her poncho, with Terelia and Gisby walking, one to each side of her, she made her way along Broadway. She was pleasantly tired — a soporific effect, Terelia had told her, needing a good nap. Instead of going all the way up to her house, she would stop at the empty apartment she had lived in above the restaurant and sleep an hour or two.

They had given her the key. She felt it in her skirt pocket, bemused by the uncompromising solidity of the metal.

"Are you all right?" Terelia asked when they came to the Mallaby Street where they would leave her and go to their own home for the Firstday afternoon siesta — and probably, Morwen thought, some inti-macy to make the sleep even more restful.

"I am fine," she said.

The couple gave her a hug each and turned toward their own house. Morwen walked on, noticing that the street seemed wider and some-how straighter, a lingering effect of the maunch.

From out of an alley between two buildings not far ahead stepped two men. Her first impression was that they were oddly dressed, both in tight singlesuits of burgundy and ocher. *Deweaseling Corps,* she thought. It was only as they came near, moving with rapid determined strides that she made the obvious connection: the colors were the livery of Hacheem Belloch. Indeed, she recognized one of them as a senior member of his pirate crew.

She had not brought the projac to the meet-up. The maunch was slowing her response time, but now she realized she needed to run. She turned, and saw a ground car pulling up to the curb beside her with another burgundy-and-ocher clad man climbing out of the passenger seat.

Farther back along the road she could see other members of the congregation. A few were walking toward her, but at a distance. Most of today's attendees, as was usual, had gathered on and below the front steps to talk. She thought she saw Eldo Kronik among them. But did he see her?

There was nowhere for Morwen to go. Two were behind her now, one in front, the street denied her by the car, and a closed shop doorway the only other direction. She tried to push past the one who had got out of the car, but immediately the pair behind seized her just above the elbows. Her arms were yanked back and she felt the cold metal of a griptight on her wrists. A bag of coarse cloth descended over her head and she felt herself lifted off her feet and carried a short distance.

She was deposited on a hard surface. The half-light inside the bag became full dark as something clicked closed above her. Then she heard the sound of the vehicle's doors closing and she was pushed back toward the rear of the luggage compartment as the car left the curb. Moments later, she was rolled in another direction as it rounded a curve. She felt it accelerate.

Still under the fading influence of maunch, Morwen remained calm, her mind still clear. Her first thought was that Belloch wanted the bead and would be disappointed to find she did not have it. But then she realized there was a more likely explanation.

She was an escaped slave. There was a reward for anyone who assisted in her recapture. There had been contact between Jerz Thanda and Belloch's representative at Interchange. Word of her whereabouts could have been passed along.

But, her lucid mind following the ramifications of that train of thought, she decided that Thanda would not do anything to complicate the auction of the hidden world. That sale was worth millions to Thanda. He could buy more ships, lay out maunch farms and mills on other worlds, and build his operation beyond anything he had previously dreamed of. He could become a power among the master criminals of the Beyond.

Besides, he did not know the password that activated the bead.

So, not Thanda. Still, there was an obvious culprit. Space ships needed maintenance. On Thanda's trips to Interchange, he had been accompanied by his new recruit, his mechanic. And Bod Hipple did not care whether Thanda's ambitions were realized or not. He did care about his own self-esteem, which Morwen had traduced. And he had seen the tattoo on her arm.

Not greed, then. Revenge.

The car had been heading downhill. Now it slowed and slewed to one side, rounding a corner. *Ring road*, Morwen thought. And soon after, it would make the turn onto the straight thoroughfare that passed the riverside Gersen farm then crossed the Parmell and ran to the east-west highway and the hotel at Brumble's Corners. That would be where they had based themselves while they scouted out her whereabouts and decided where to make the snatch.

That would be where their space ship had put down, one of the liveried vehicles in Belloch's colors. It would have disgorged the car and the four henchmen, then gone somewhere else — very likely into a stationary orbit — so it could come down when called and pick them up. Or it might be hovering overhead right now. Probably, the car would drive aboard, and the next time Morwen saw light, she would be out in space.

On her way to her reckoning with Hacheem Belloch, who thought it good management to make unforgettable examples of slaves who tried to escape his grasp. But first her captors would amuse themselves with her on the voyage back to Blatcher's World. No doubt, Bod Hipple would enjoy the thought of that.

The car turned onto the straight road and accelerated again. Morwen considered her situation. The bag over her head was loose. If she drubbed her head against the floor of the luggage compartment, she could get it off her. About the griptight, she could do nothing, but her legs and feet were unrestrained. She could kick. She could run. Given enough space, she could even manage a flying kick.

It wasn't much of an arsenal of weapons, but it was all she had. She began to twist about. Hunched over, she could manage to get to her knees. When they opened the compartment lid, she could spring out and see what damage she could do. If all else failed, they might have to kill her to stop her.

The car swerved, oddly making it easier for her to get to a kneeling position. Then it swerved again, more sharply, and she was thrown onto her side. *Do they know?* she thought. *Are they doing that to throw me down?*

Another swerve, a sudden braking, then a jerk that pushed her up against the wall beyond which were the backs of the rear seats. She heard muffled shouting, someone yelling, "Faster!" and another voice responding with a foul curse.

Then there came a thump and a sudden sense of weightlessness. *We're airborne,* Morwen managed to think, before the car slammed to earth again and tilted sharply sideways. Now she could hear the sound of something scraping against the vehicle's bottom and she put that down to their having left the road to slide along a ditch.

But she knew the ditches on this road were interrupted by culverts that helped prevent flooding during the rainy season. And no sooner had Morwen realized this than the car came to a smashing halt and she was thrown again, this time bruisingly hard, against the rear seatbacks.

She heard shouting, doors opening and slamming, followed by the unmistakable *zivv* sound of projac beams igniting the air of their passage. Then the eerie shriek of a disorganizer.

Someone was shouting orders. Another discharge from the disorganizer, and all fell quiet. Morwen waited, her still strangely lucid brain putting together a sequence of events to explain what she had heard.

Then came a grate of metal on metal as someone applied a tool to the compartment lid, causing it to fly up and show her an expanse of blue sky, broken by the silhouette of Eldo Kronik, looking down at her.

"Are you all right?" he said.

"All is well," she said.

He helped her out of the broken ground car and up and out of the dry ditch. Two bodies lay sprawled in the road, the burgundy and ocher singlesuits showing charred gaps where their flesh had been penetrated by projac beams. Nearby was a puddle of gray and pink semi-liquid, lumpy with what looked like elements of a semi-digested meal. Morwen had never seen the effects of a disorganizer, but had read descriptions in those tales of derring-do. She was glad of the lingering vapors of the maunch, which kept her from being overwhelmed by the sight.

Kronik was unfastening the griptight. She shook her freed wrists. Two of his deputies were marching the fourth of Belloch's pirates, his wrists bound as Morwen's had been, toward an air car hovering above the field flanking the road. A deputy in the skyrider was powering down a mounted disorganizer, its work done.

"I didn't know you had an air car," she said to Kronik. She looked up into the bright sky, but saw no sign of a space ship in Belloch's colors.

"Not much need for it," he said. "Except when there is."

A constabulary ground car was coming down from New Dispensation. "We'll get you back home and make sure you're all right," Kronik said. "Then I'll have a talk with that fellow and find out what this was all about."

"He'll be more afraid of his employer than of you," Morwen said. "But I can tell you who was behind this."

The deputies pushed the bodies off to the side of the road but left the pool of disorganized protoplasm where it lay. Hoppers were not known to be picky in their feeding habits.

"We didn't go up the hill to arrest Hipple," the scrutineer told her later, when he stopped by to check on her. "The Covenant reserves punishment of Protectors to the Corporation. We'll let Thanda deal with him."

She was sitting in her kitchen, drinking a herbal tea whose flavor reminded her of the maunch. She offered him some and he accepted a cup, although she guessed it was not his usual beverage.

"He'll be gone," she said. Her feelings on the matter surprised her. Hipple had meant to do her harm, but she didn't care. She supposed her equanimity was one of the lingering effects of the sacrament. All was well.

She looked at Kronik, the hard-planed face, the piercing eyes, the reluctant smile.

He was still beautiful.

Chapter Six

Begby Horth opted not to participate in the auction. Hacheem Belloch decided he would take part. The seven bidders, each with an entourage, came to Hambledon spaceport in their own ships. A convoy of air cars had been arranged by Jerz Thanda to collect them and take them directly to the Manse. Here the senior criminals shed their followers and, so they declared, any personal weapons carried on their persons, and boarded the Itinerator III.

Eldo Kronik brought Morwen up from the town, the encrypted bead in his possession. She looked around to see if she could spot Bod Hipple among the Protectors ringing the launch pad. She could not, nor was he aboard the yacht when she boarded.

She found that she was expected to use her culinary skills during the voyage, but she did not mind. She could spend her time in the galley, performing functions that were familiar to her, and not have to associate with the criminals who took over the saloon and the plush staterooms farther forward in the ship.

The bidders were:

Malvo Krick, owner of gaming facilities on several worlds in the Beyond, who affected the guise of a jolly fat man, though his eyes belied the smiles and laughter;

Thatch Parnassian, whose organization bought and sold stolen property, from individual pieces of jewelry to the contents of entire warehouses; often his customers were the victims from whom the goods had been taken, or their insurers; he was a slim and quiet man, as cold and watchful, Morwen thought, as a predatory reptile;

Petrof Ban Khediv, whose line of business was space ships, which he bought cheap from anyone who had acquired one — pirates and individual thieves, mostly — then reconfigured them, gave them false papers, and sold them to buyers in both the Oikumene and the Beyond; he was large and grim, and it was said no one had ever seen him smile;

Sheleen Two Hearts, a slaver who dealt in human flesh but could get a customer an ultraterrene, though with no guarantees the alien creature would long survive captivity; unlike Khediv, he wore a perpetual grin and was known for his practical jokes, usually inventive, sometimes fatal;

Shug Fornister, who had started out his career as hired muscle but had parlayed his cold-blooded skills into a murder-for-pay organization, with a strong sideline in kidnapping, the victims redeemed through Interchange; he was the image of a hired killer — neat, methodical, and without discernible emotion;

Jander Bao, a genius of a fraudster who created appealing fantasies into which marks on several of the Oikumene worlds jostled each other to invest their funds, never to see the promised fabulous earnings; he affected the appearance of a friendly neighbor, always ready to do a good turn; and, finally,

Hacheem Belloch, pirate and Morwen's ostensible owner, cool and reserved when in company, though savage when he was about his business; he was believed to have subjected several freighter crews to a cold walk in space, then sold their cargoes to Parnassian and their ships to Khediv.

Kronik told Morwen that Belloch understood that one intent of the sale of the hidden world was to buy her parents out of slavery and recognize her emancipation.

"And how did he receive that news?" she asked.

"With a grunt."

"Then he may not comply."

Kronik said the other bidders were aware of the side deal and did not want anything to disrupt their plans.

"Parnassian and Khediv have reminded him that there are other pirates they can deal with. Fornister spoke only a few words, but left a clear impression that interference with the auction would leave him disconsolate."

Morwen was heartened by these reassurances, but resolved to keep a watchful eye on her former keeper. Kronik had smuggled her projac aboard and slipped it to her. She resolved to keep it within easy reach.

Once they had lifted off from Providence, she and Kronik had gone to the cockpit and placed the bead in the ship's reader. She had whispered the nonsense password and seen the ship accept the heading and begin to accelerate into the immensity. She retrieved the bead and handed it to Kronik, who placed it in the yacht's safe, the combination to which he had reset. Before it would open, it would also require his thumbprint to touch a sensor.

And so they all ate the meal she had prepared — she dining alone in her cabin — then Thanda engaged the intersplit and they slipped into nonspace.

None of the seven, nor Thanda, brought their plates back to the galley. Morwen went forward to collect them, and found Thanda and six of the bidders playing a card game. The exception was Shug Fornister, who stood alone, staring at the forward viewing screen, which displayed the irreality that surrounded the ship when the intersplit was active. But Morwen thought he was seeing other images in his mind — images that she doubted she or any other normal human being would want to witness.

She went around the saloon, gathering plates into a stack. The card players ignored her, even when she plucked a dish from under the elbow of one of them. But when she was directly across the table from him, Hacheem Belloch raised his eyes from his cards and fixed her with a chilling gaze. She had to repress a lifelong impulse to abase herself before him.

"You cost me four men," he said, in a tone that he could have used to discuss mild weather.

She had to force herself to meet his eyes. "Three," she said. "One is in custody."

"Four," he said. "I don't reward failure. The overseer who let you escape could tell you that." He rearranged a card in his hand. "Except he's not in a position to tell anybody anything. So that makes five."

She waited until she could be sure her voice would not quaver. "The deal is, you deliver my parents, I pay the ransom. I'm told you keep deals."

He stared at her, deadpan. "The deal says nothing about what kind of shape they're in."

"If you harm them, the deal is off. I will destroy the bead and that will be the end of it."

She hadn't heard Fornister speak before. His voice was even milder than Belloch's feigned calm. "Hacheem, you don't want to let your feelings mess this up. People will remember that."

Belloch turned to look at the killer-for-hire, who continued to regard the intersplit mysteries that filled the viewing screen. "Are you threatening me?" he said.

"I never threaten anybody," Fornister said. "Threatening is not the business I'm in."

Sheleen Two Hearts spoke now, as he discarded one card and took another from the deck. "Give the woman her parents and take the money," he advised Hacheem. "You don't want to make enemies."

Belloch's eyes widened. He glared at the man across the table. Two Hearts considered his new card and said, "Raise you a thousand."

Morwen went back to the galley. The plates were clattering softly in her shaking hands.

"All will be well," she told herself.

They came back into normal space, and there was the vast cloud before them. The ship knew its way and took them through it at more speed than the first time, the gas slithering along the hull and superstructure, hissing like a pit of serpents. They burst out into the open, the white dwarf hanging in the blackness like a pinprick in a dark curtain, its planets neither beckoning nor warning-off, but just *there*.

Again, they orbited the little world, the bidders taking turns at the macroscope, then spiraled down to land on the planet's single prominence. The seven trooped out onto the narrow, triangular flat space with the sheer drops on all sides, then scattered in different directions to take their impressions of the world. They mooched about, kicked at clumps of moss in crevices, gazed out over the sullen sea, sniffed the cold, wet air.

Belloch was the first back on board. He went to sit in the warmth of the saloon and drew a mug of punge from the pot kept warming there. The others came back, one by one, took seats or leaned against the walls.

Jander Bao said, "You could take off the top of this spire, down to where it's wider, and have room for a substantial house."

"It would be a damp and chilly house," said Thatch Parnassian, contorting his face into a grimace.

"Nobody's buying this place for comforts," said Malvo Krick.

"Let's go," said Belloch. "Get this done."

The yacht lifted off and climbed out of the wet air, nosed into the gas cloud, and found its way back to the Beyond. Thanda removed the monitor's coding strip and jettisoned it out the airlock. He set a course for Sasani and engaged the intersplit.

Morwen retired to her cabin, locked the door, and sat on the bunk, cradling her projac.

When they were within range, Thanda communicated with Interchange. A multi-seated air car was waiting for them at the spaceport. They climbed into the charabanc and it went aloft and took them across the desert in far more comfort than the airship and decrepit bus could have managed. At Interchange, they set down at a different compound, where screens and sonic barriers kept the biting insects at a distance. They followed a guide to a building where a lectern sat atop a podium before which were ranged seven chairs in a demilune.

A soft-faced senior manager awaited them. He wore formal attire, with a gold badge in the shape of Interchange's clasped hands on his left lapel. He introduced himself as Hyron Debonshar. He would be the auctioneer. Kronik handed him the encrypted bead while the bidders took their seats and Kronik, Thanda, and Morwen stood to one side of the podium.

Debonshar regarded the bead for a moment then placed it on the top of the lectern. He cast his gaze over the seven and said, "We will proceed. Are all of you in agreement with the terms?"

The bidders replied with nods or yesses. Thatch Parnassian said, "Get on with it."

"I will begin with a floor price of ten million svu," said the auction-eer, "then increase by one million increments until we have a winner."

Hearing no dissent, he said, "Ten million. Do I hear eleven?"

Hacheem Belloch was the first to raise his hand.

"I have eleven," said Debonshar. "Do I hear twelve?"

Malvo Krick signaled that was his bid.

And so it went, the numbers rising. At twenty million svu, Par-nassian dropped out, followed not long after by Khediv. Before the bidding reached thirty million, Belloch, Bao, and Fornister had quit.

Malvo Krick and Sheleen Two Hearts remained in contention. Debonshar increased the bids by five million. At forty million, Krick made a pushing-away gesture.

"Sold to Sheleen Two Hearts," said Debonshar. "As a matter of per-sonal curiosity, may I ask the origin of your name?"

Two Hearts showed that he would take offense if the issue was pressed. Jander Bao said, "Among his people, names are earned by notable deeds. Ser Two Hearts is a notable duelist, even more notable for having consumed the hearts of two of those who unsuccessfully met him on the field of honor."

Hyron Debonshar's plump visage tinted a little green. Two Hearts smiled to show he did not mind hearing himself thus described. He advanced to the podium, took from an inner pocket of his upper garment a sheaf of bank drafts, sorted among them until he had put together four, then added a fifth. These he turned over to Hyron Debonshar, who recovered his equanimity and examined them closely, before tucking them into a purse he wore slung on a leather strap that crossed his torso from shoulder to waist.

He handed Two Hearts the encrypted bead. The slaver examined it, then beckoned to Morwen to follow him into a far corner of the room. She went, though bumps of chilled flesh rose on her limbs despite the warmth of the room in a desert.

Two Hearts produced a hand-held reader and placed the bead in its receptacle. To Morwen he said, "Whisper the password in my ear," and turned his head.

A bone passed through the lobe of his ear. It looked like it had come from a human finger. Repressing revulsion, she did as he bade her.

"Again," he said, and she repeated the nonsense syllables.

Two Hearts put his mouth close to the device and whispered the word himself. The reader generated a small screen and filled it with figures. The pirate lord studied them for a moment, then without a word, he shut off the device, turned, and walked toward the door.

Morwen went to where the Interchange manager stood in quiet conversation with Thanda. "What of my arrangements?" she said.

"All is in hand," the man said. "Ser Belloch has accepted the terms. The persons in question will be brought here by our staff, the fees will be rescinded from funds now on deposit, and the documents of manumission executed."

"You're sure?" she said.

"Young woman," Debonshar said, visibly bridling, "this is Interchange. When we say a thing will be done, it will be done."

Eldo Kronik had come up behind her. "Sera Morwen has some understandable anxiety," he said. "Her parents' experience of this place made for an unhappy impression."

Debonshar made a sound that said he was only partly mollified, but turned to a subject he found more pleasant. To Thanda, he said, "Your funds are now liquid, less our commission. If you wish, we would be happy to advise you on investment possibilities."

Thanda smiled. "My plans are already well thought out."

Debonshar showed the face of a man who has done his duty to his employer. He turned back to Morwen and said, "As a rescinder of fees, we can offer you Class-B accommodation and meals until the business is completed."

Class-B accommodations consisted of a small room with a bed, a minimal ablutory, and a chair. The food was whatever insipid meals were served in the Class-B cafeteria, populated by "guests" waiting with various degrees of optimism or despair for their "fees" to be "rescinded." In any other locale, they would have been "kidnap victims or hostages" waiting for their "ransoms" to be "paid." Those who were not redeemed would, after a set period, be priced according to their market value and offered for sale to whoever was willing to pay.

Mostly, that would be a dealer in slaves. Some of the guests had been taken from wealthy worlds in the Oikumene and would be ransomed if their families or employers considered them worth the demanded sum. Others were stolen out of their lives in ill-defended communities on worlds in the Beyond. A few had been passengers or crew on space ships that had been stopped and boarded by pirates, usually in some star system where traffic was heavy enough to have a choice of targets.

Morwen's tattoo drew attention if she failed to keep it out of sight. Some of the "guests" asked her questions about the life of slavery and she answered as truthfully as she could without encouraging suicide. But mostly she avoided contact with the detainees and kept to her small room, staring at the featureless walls or sleeping several hours out of the day.

At least once a day she would approach one of the junior managers who oversaw the cafeteria operations and ask it there was any news of her parents. The answer was always a variation on *in good time.*

Then one day she was awakened from a day-time nap by a brisk knock on the door. As she sat up, it opened and a man in Interchange uniform said she was to come immediately. He had no other information to give her, but she followed him through locked doors then down corridors, out of the "guest" quarters and across a courtyard to an administrative block, and finally to a closed door that bore a letter and a number.

The man left her there, indicating that she should proceed alone. Morwen took a deep, settling breath, then knocked and pushed the portal aside. Behind the door was a nondescript chamber with chairs against the walls. As she entered, two persons rose from the chairs and looked at her with astonishment that soon became joy.

But her mother's happiness faded to fear. "Morwen," she said, "are you taken? After all the waiting…"

"No, mother," she said. "I am free and so are you."

Now came the tears. Her father said, "They told us nothing. Just get dressed, get aboard the ship, remain where you are put, and ask no questions."

"We thought we had been sold on," Elva said, "someplace you would never be able to find us."

"We will never be separated again," Morwen said.

And then, for a while, there were only tears and endearments, until the messenger returned bearing documents. "Here are your manumission papers from Blatcher's World, a statement of account for our fees and services, and —" he handed Morwen a wad of high-denomination SVU certificates "— the unspent balance of the funds deposited to your account. Which is now closed."

He led the three of them to the discharging area, where Morwen's projac was returned to her. The old bus was waiting and they ran through the insect attack to get aboard. They sat in the rear seats and she noticed her parents' watchfulness: the constant awareness of slaves taken out of their normal milieu that their behavior might be noticed and bring punishment.

That will take some time to get over, she thought. *Perhaps the maunch would help.*

The driver climbed aboard, along with a redeemed "guest" and the functionary his employer had sent to pay his "fees." The door closed, then the bus rumbled to life and left Interchange.

A few days later, aboard a different omnibus, the three Morwens arrived outside the Llanko Inn in what had been Mount Pleasant. Chaffe and Elva stepped down from the vehicle carrying the few things they had bought at the Sasani spaceport and gazed around as if they had been transported to the contents of a dream.

The bus pulled away revealing a hard-faced man in a black and gray uniform crossing the street from the town hall. Morwen's parents flinched, their heads drawing into their hunched shoulders.

"It's all right," their daughter said. "He's a friend."

Eldo Kronik put on the best smile of which he was able and welcomed them home. "I'll escort you," he said, indicating the white and blue woodframe house halfway up the big hill.

Morwen glanced that way and saw a barrier on the switchback above the old house, attended by men in black and blue uniforms. She looked a question at Kronik, and he said, "Changes while you were away. Jerz Thanda has hired new Protectors — a lot of them — now that he has more to protect."

Again, he gestured to Mount Pleasant. Morwen raised her gaze to the Manse and saw three space ships on the pad outside the stone pile, and a busyness of machinery and people next to them.

"More ships, a new pad, and fortifications to protect them," Kronik said. "Plus a new barracks block for the fresh recruits. I think he is also installing military-grade weapons from the Oikumene."

Morwen knew that the settled worlds of the more civilized reach of the galactic arm had long ago disbanded their militaries. Perpetual abundance and the practical impossibilities of one world succeeding in dominating another had done away with the idea of conquest. "Where did he get such things?" she said.

"Museums, perhaps," Kronik said as they crossed the street to where his ground car waited. "Although some speculate that the Institute works to slow down the development of new technologies. Their goal is to manage change so that it moves forward at a creeping pace, allowing those in charge — who are often Institute trained — to control our lives.

"But when it comes to old technologies, the Institute has retained all the plans and specifications for what has gone before — even weapons of war from the days when megalomaniac loons dreamed that interplanetary war was feasible, let alone desirable. So, it is just a matter of purchasing a factory, feeding the information into its systems, stocking the raw materials, and pressing the on button."

He drove the car onto the first of the switchbacks. As they climbed the slopes, Morwen saw the activity atop the hill in more detail. She also got a clearer view of the gate and guardhouse just above the level of her house. Black-and-blue uniformed men watched as the constabulary car approached, their attitudes alert, until Kronik turned off and parked beside the house.

"You're home," he said. "I took the liberty of stocking your larder with fresh stuff. Also the crib is gone and there's a bed in the second room."

Morwen hugged him. It felt like the natural thing to do, though he at first didn't respond. But he put his arms around her and held her lightly, saying — she thought, to himself — "All right."

Then he left them.

Chaffe and Elva Sabine looked about them, still seeming to be half in a dream. The sun was westering, throwing shadows on the streets of the town below, and lighting golden blazes in all the greenhouses — of which Morwen was sure there were now even more than before.

"Let's go in," she said.

She did not go to work for a few days, spending the time with her parents. The fact that they had been brought back to the place from which they were stolen probably increased their sense of inhabiting a dream, it seemed to her. But, at the same time, they had been transported to a setting they were familiar with, even if it had also been transformed.

Her mother noticed the fresh grave below the front porch. "Mumpsimus?" she said.

"I'm afraid so," Morwen said.

Elva Sabine bent over the little mound of earth and watered it with a tear.

On the third day, when they appeared more rested, she took them down to meet Gisby and Terelia. Again, it must have been a strange experience to be back in their restaurant, though it was no longer theirs. Chaffe and Elva moved about the place, touching things here and there, stopping at moments to stare at some detail and superimpose upon it the memory of twenty-five years ago.

The thing that struck Morwen most strongly was the sense of inertia that hung over her parents like a fog. She realized it was the legacy of decades in servitude. In the household of Hacheem Belloch, there had been no doubt as to what a slave had to do. Routines were well established and expectations high. Woe betide a bondsman found lollygagging, as Vilch the overseer would have put it. The least that would have followed would have been a buffet to the side of the head or a kick to the buttocks. But if Vilch felt the need for a general stimulus, the entire complement of house and estate ground would have been assembled to witness a whipping.

In New Dispensation, there was no Vilch, no whipping post. Her parents would need to be motivated by attributes that had naturally atrophied during their sojourn in involuntary servitude. *So*, she told herself, *I had better find them work.*

The restaurant couldn't employ them. It didn't do enough business. They were a chef and a cook, unlikely to adapt to new occupations at their age and after what they had been through. A brief period of thought brought Morwen to the only logical solution. Leaving her parents at home, she mounted her bicycle and turned it uphill.

The guards at the checkpoint stopped her. She knew one of them; the others were new hires.

"What do you want?" said the one with three stripes on his cuff, one of the newcomers.

"I want to see Jerz Thanda."

"What for?"

She rested on the bike's seat and met the man's gaze. "Does he discuss his business with you?"

The man frowned and hitched up his belt. At this point, the old hire said, "The Commander knows her. She's the one who went to Interchange with him."

His superior didn't like having to give ground. On the other hand, rousting someone Thanda valued could cost a man a stripe — or worse. He found a solution by tapping his communicator and speaking a few words into it. Then they waited. Finally, the device beeped and the guard put it to his ear. A moment later, he said, "Raise the gate."

At the manse, Morwen was led through a series of rooms, once the parlors and retiring chambers of the Prophet Armbruch, now occupied by men and women sitting at desks and long tables, their attention on screens and keyboards. Beyond this hive of activity, she found Thanda in his office, his own integrator on the fine old desk behind which he sat in a chair that was only one step removed from a throne. The room had once been the private chamber of the aristocrat who had brought the first colonists to Mount Pleasant back in the fourteen hundreds. His books still stood on the shelves of a glass-fronted cabinet behind Thanda. Morwen could read some of the titles: *Life*, a multivolume work by the renowned philosopher Unspiek, Baron Bodissey, of whom she had heard, and a slim volume bound in pink chamois by someone named Navarth, of whom she had not.

Thanda gave her a considering look and waved her to a chair. "What do you want?"

Morwen had decided on an approach. "You remember when we were on the yacht?"

"I'm not likely to forget it."

"You liked my cooking."

She saw that the conversation was veering off from Thanda's expectations, but he let her lead it wherever it was going. "I did. Are you applying for a job?"

She shook her head. "No, I'm recommending someone for a job. Two someones. The two someones who taught me everything I know about what to do in a kitchen."

Now Thanda saw where they had arrived. "Ah," he said.

"You know they can't be weasels," she said, "not after where they've been."

"Granted."

Morwen leaned forward, pressed her point. "Also, you've come up in the world. You can afford the attributes of gracious living. Hacheem Belloch expected gourmet meals. My parents survived more than twenty years of his expectations."

"'The attributes of gracious living.' It has a ring to it," Thanda said. He paused and stared at her, and she sensed his mind working.

When he didn't answer, she said, "Well?"

He looked about the office, then came back to zero in on her. "I remember more than your cooking," he said.

Now it was her turn not to know where things were going. She showed him a face that said as much. He leaned back in his great chair and interlaced his fingers, studying her again.

"I remember how you were with those pirates and killers," he said. "You dealt with them, right in their faces."

"I was scared," she said.

"So was I," he said, "but I saw it through." He made a face that told her a salient point was coming next. "And so did you."

"What are we doing here?" Morwen said.

"We're about to discuss the concept of your coming to work for me."

She showed him the palms of both hands. "I've got a job. It's my parents who need something to do."

"I'll give your people a job, if you come, too."

She smiled and shook her head, saying, "You know the old saying about too many cooks."

Thanda leaned forward, his face serious. "I don't want you to cook," he said.

The answer flummoxed her. After a moment to recover, she said, "You're not thinking that…you and I. I mean, I'm already involved, sort of—"

He gave a half-snort. "Not that. And I know about you and the brave scrutineer who saved you from the nasty snatchers."

"Then what?" Morwen said.

Thanda's left forefinger ticked off items on his right hand. "You're tough. You're smart. You don't take your eye off the target. You adapt to changing circumstances and you see the job through to the end."

Now he closed that hand and made a fist, showed it to her. "I want you to be my right hand."

Morwen was having trouble seeing what he was seeing. "What would I have to do?"

"Whatever needed doing. Mostly thinking. And especially double-checking me when I am working through an issue."

She blinked at him. "This is not what I expected."

"If my assessment of you is correct," Thanda said, "you'll adjust to the situation and make the right decision."

Eldo Kronik said, "I see you don't wear the uniform."

Morwen said, "I don't think of myself as one of his Protectors."

The scrutineer made his face an invitation for her to say more.

"I'm an adviser," she said. "Sometimes I am tasked with resolving a specific situation, but mostly I'm there to keep an eye on things and think about whether they're going the right way."

They were sitting in his office at the constabulary. Morwen had dropped in to make sure all the documentation for her parents' residency in New Dispensation was in order. Since the massive inflow of funds into the maunch extract business, now augmented by the largesse Thanda had brought back from Interchange, the community had been attracting new residents. There were now no longer any vacant properties, and the Llanko Inn was filled to capacity. Builders had come in from Hambledon and other settlements to put up new houses — all owned by Thanda's operation, now formally established as the New Dispensation Development Corporation. Morwen was on the company's books as "Senior Adviser to the Managing Directorate."

"What you are," said Kronik, "is Jerz Thanda's effectuator. Less politely, his fixer."

"This bothers you?" Morwen said.

He looked out the window at the activity atop the hill. A second new barracks block was being erected by heavy machines that extruded walls in liquid stone that soon colloided into solid form. Then he looked back at her. "Not if it doesn't bother you."

"I needed something to do," she said.

"And you didn't know you needed it until Thanda opened a door and showed you what lay beyond."

He was right. She had done some thinking after Thanda made his offer, and before she accepted it. She had spent her whole life, from early childhood to young adulthood, training for a specific goal then, whenever the opportunity presented, taking a step or two toward it.

Now, in her mid-twenties, she had achieved that goal: complete success, every aspect fulfilled. And that raised the question: what next? What do you do when you've accomplished your life's work, with decades of time still stretching out before you?

She could be a cook in a small-town restaurant, albeit a small town that was growing at a boom-town rate. She could have invested her remaining funds in some greenhouses and planted maunch; plenty of Dispers were making their fortunes that way. Or she could start a business of her own, though in truth the only skill she had was cookery — except, of course, for the abilities and qualities Thanda had seen in her.

"The main thing," he said, as he watched her mull those thoughts, "is if you're happy."

"That is a novel consideration," she said, after a moment. "All my life, I could ask myself if what I was doing was bringing me closer to the goal. Whether or not I was happy was an irrelevance."

"But now...?" Kronik prompted.

She confirmed his thought with a nod. "Now it's something to be added to the recipe."

"Which makes for a different flavor, doesn't it?"

"I'm getting used to the taste," she said. "But back to the other question: you don't mind my working for Thanda?"

"Not if it's only work," he said.

"It would never be anything else."

He glanced again at the bustle atop the hill, and said, "My allegiance is to the community. I swore an oath to protect and defend it, and I take oaths seriously. Jerz Thanda is a reality. He has an impact on New Dispensation, in fact, a range of impacts."

His lips pursed as he reflected then he said, "Some of those impacts have been hurtful to a few. The Prophet's death may not bear looking into. But before Thanda came, this town was on the road to dissolution. We would have died happy — maunch has the quality of smoothing out life's rough spots — but in the end there would have been a handful of us chewing and chasing our visions.

"Now we are prosperous, growing, there are new families coming in. And I would say we are a happy place, as I gather Mount Pleasant was before the raid."

"You should ask my parents about it, sometime," Morwen said. "Though to them it is more like a dream remembered from childhood." She would not recommend he talk to Dedana Llanko. The old woman's horrific memories were almost as bad as the worst of Morwen's.

"I might, some day," Kronik said, "when they're … a little stronger."

"They're getting better. Thanda has let it be known they are not just servants."

She saw Kronik's half-smile come and go. "And, of course, nobody wants to cross his fixer."

She let that go. Instead, she said, "There is a dance on Fifthday. Were you thinking of going?"

"I might," he said. "You?"

She got up and headed for the door, saying over her shoulder, "I might."

Up at the Manse, she had an office next to Thanda's, with a desk and a communicator and an integrator. Papers came her way, reports and projections on extract production, the fluctuations of markets on worlds in the Beyond and the Oikumene, the rise and fall of prices.

Thanda had given her a couple of tutorials and her natural intelligence was deepening her understanding of markets and economic forces.

Morwen was gratified to learn that Thanda's interest was solely focused on maunch and its extract. He did not see himself extending into other spheres of criminality, like extortion or lending money at usurious rates and collecting by thuggish methods. She reckoned his aversion was not moral, but on a recognition that varying his lines of business would bring him into conflict with already established operations that would resent the competition. Such resentment would be expressed in violence.

On the other hand, with maunch and its extract, the New Dispensation Development Corporation had a monopoly on production and a distribution network already in place. The business was established and lucrative. Prices for the two products were highest on those worlds of the Oikumene where the cultures eschewed the use of mind-altering substances. Their local police forces — sometimes community-specific, sometimes planet-wide — sought to quell the traffic, and coordinated their efforts with the IPCC, but demand kept rising. And Thanda was meeting that demand with increased supply.

It bemused Morwen to think that, if she stepped onto one of those worlds to do Thanda's business, she would be a criminal. But, then, she had heard of a world where she would face possible arrest, or at least a ticket and fine, for showing her knees or elbows. And another where, in at least one region, an unaccompanied woman was assumed to be willing to perform salacious conduct for a fee. In that region, the conduct was not prohibited, nor the transactional nature, but its practice without a license and certificate of health was punishable by a fine and imprisonment. If she walked the streets alone there, she would be continually stopped and required to display documents she did not possess.

She sorted through the papers that had come across her desk while she had been visiting Eldo Kronik, triaging them into those that needed immediate attention, those that could wait, and those that she needed only initial and pass on. She made some notes, wrote a brief memo of recommendation on one pressing issue, and signed off on the irrelevancies.

MATTHEW HUGHES

Then she turned her attention to a matter that had been nagging at her ever since she had joined Thanda's establishment. The officer in charge of personnel was in his office, down a corridor. She went, knocked on his door, and entered without being invited.

A balding man with a chin beard looked up from the papers on his desk as she came in and closed the door. His voice was studiedly neutral. "How may I help you?"

"Bod Hipple," she said, placing her palms on the desk and leaning toward him.

He automatically drew back. Morwen was becoming good at the mechanics of exercising power.

"What of him?"

"Exactly," she said. "What became of him?"

"I don't know. Nobody knows."

She made a beckoning gesture with one hand, to show that she needed more information. The personnel chief sighed. "He disappeared. He didn't give in a resignation. Just one day, he wasn't here anymore."

Morwen straightened. "Not a weasel?"

The man shook his head. "Born on Tantamount. Came here as an infant with the rest of the colony and was raised by good Dispers. Took over his father's repair business when the old man went into maunch farming."

"When exactly did he disappear?" Morwen asked.

"Don't know, but…" A ledger was opened, a page found, a finger moved down to land on a listing. "He collected his pay here." He turned the book to show her the date. "That was the last anyone saw of him."

Morwen looked. The date was two days before Belloch's men attempted to seize her.

"Did we look for him?" she said.

"Yes, in all the usual places."

"What about the spaceport?"

"He'd never shown any interest in going offworld."

Morwen gave the matter some thought then asked, "Theory?"

The personnel chief's brow furrowed. "He was unhappy about something. A personal thing. But he made no close friends here, nobody he

thing. A personal thing. But he made no close friends here, nobody he

— 118 —

would confide in. A loner, but good with engines. Not good at taking orders.

"We figured he'd gone somewhere he felt more comfortable. There are plenty of settlements on Providence where a mechanic can have a good life."

"Huh," said Morwen. She thanked him and went back to her desk, where she sat and rolled a stylus around between thumb and two fingers. After a while, she knocked on the connecting door to Thanda's office and went in.

He put down the paper he had been studying and showed her an expectant face.

"I need to sign out a ground car," she said.

"Then do so. What's it about?"

"I don't know yet. Maybe a problem. Maybe nothing. I'll find out."

Thanda took up the paper again. "That's what you're here for."

Chapter Seven

The Brumble Hotel looked no different. Morwen parked near the front steps and went up. It was early afternoon and there were only a few drinkers in the common room. The owner was not on the scene, but Maddie was stacking mugs and glasses behind the bar.

"Got a minute?" Morwen said.

"Sure," the young woman said, "and I've got something to tell you." At Morwen's questioning look, Maddie said, "Some offworlders were here a while back, four of them, with a picture of you. I told them I didn't recognize the face, but Brumble blabbed."

"Hmm," said Morwen. She brought out the image of Bod Hipple that had been used to make his Protector identification card. "How about this fellow?"

Maddie glanced at it. "Couldn't forget those jug ears," she said. "He was here at the same time. Didn't come in, though. But I saw him talking to the four in the parking lot, before they came in."

"Did you hear what they were saying?"

"No." Maddie shook her head, then added, "But there's something else."

"What?"

"Those offworlders didn't come on the omnibus."

"I know," Morwen said. "They had a ground car."

The young woman held up a hand to make a point. "That's not all they had. They had a space ship. Their car came out of its main hatch."

"What happened to the ship?"

"They left Mr. Big Ears to look after it. I saw him standing out there, looking toward New Dispensation. Then I got busy and, next time I looked, he was gone and so was the ship. It never made a sound, coming or going, by the way."

Morwen took out her wallet, gave Maddie a five-SVU certificate. "You don't need to do that," Maddie said.

"I want to," Morwen said. "And if anybody lands another ship here, especially one that makes no noise, will you call me?"

"Sure. How?"

Morwen took the communicator from her pocket and handed it over. "Hold down this button and say, 'Morwen' and you'll get me."

"Will do," said Maddie. She tucked the device out of sight.

"And don't do anything else. Those men were dangerous."

"Were?"

"Three of them are dead. One is breaking rocks in Chorestown. And I'm going to find Mr. Big Ears."

Chorestown's real name was the Hambledon Penal Colony. Its operating philosophy was that inmates sent there from communities in a wide surrounding area would benefit from not having too many idle hours — or, indeed, any. The Colony hosted several businesses: a farm, a textile factory, a gravel mill.

In the latter, hard-core inmates sentenced to hard labor used sledgehammers to break large boulders into fist-sized rocks that were loaded into a crushing mill. The end product was carried on conveyor belts to form wide-based conical mounds of gravel that could be sold to municipal road-builders and private construction outfits. The New Dispensation Development Corporation had bought many truckloads for its expansion projects.

The gravel mill employed the most recalcitrant convicts, mostly those who'd had life-long difficulty conforming to other people's expectation of proper behavior. When Morwen drove onto the site and stopped at the razor-fence, she could see several men at work with hammers on a slew of gray rocks that had been blasted out of a cliff face.

She'd asked Eldo Kronik to call ahead for her, so the guard detail were expecting her. One of them, with a double chevron on the front of his peaked cap, approached as she got out of the car. "You wanted Bazzo, right?"

"I never knew his name. He'd have come from New Dispensation a little while back."

"We don't know his name, either, so we gave him one that fits," the guard said. "He never says a word." He looked over at the men swinging hammers. "You might be wasting your time."

"Might be," Morwen said. "Still got to try."

"Go in the hut. We'll bring him along."

Morwen sat behind a table in the guard's shack. Time passed. Eventually, she heard the clink of chains and the door opened. She recognized the man as the survivor of the kidnap attempt, and he recognized her.

He came in with two guards, his wrists and ankles fettered, and both connected by cables to a chain about his waist. There was a fresh bruise on his cheek.

The double-chevron guard gestured with a shock-stick toward the chair opposite Morwen. "Sit."

The two guards stood back, but not too far. "We should stay," the senior man said.

"You can if you want," she said. She took out her projac and put it within easy reach on the table. "But he knows I'd just as soon kill him as look at him. I don't think he'll make trouble. He thinks he's going to get out of here."

That brought her a hard stare from the manacled pirate. Morwen gave him back the same unflinching gaze. The guards watched them for a moment, then the senior man said, "Let's go."

When they were alone, Morwen continued to meet the prisoner's stare. When she felt it had gone on long enough, she said, "Belloch will not send anyone to free you."

No response from across the table.

Morwen said, "I went to Interchange with him. You were mentioned as having survived the kidnap attempt. His response, and I quote him exactly, 'I do not reward failure.' You know what happened to the overseer who failed to prevent my escape."

The pirate didn't quite blink, but she saw a flicker in his eyes.

"Problem is, if he sends someone to look for you, he's going to hear that you spent this time with me in private. Maybe you told me what I wanted to know, maybe you didn't."

The man's eyes narrowed involuntarily.

"That's right," Morwen said. "Whether you did or didn't, Belloch's response will be the same. You know him, and I know him. I spent almost all of my life in his household."

She waited now, not expecting the man to speak, but just letting the thought of what his employer would do fill his mind.

When the silence had gone on long enough, she said, "But I could get you out of here. I could get you out of the Beyond. New papers, some money, transportation to a civilized world where you could get lost among the billions."

She let another silence fill the room, the only sound that of hammers hitting rock. After a while, the rock crusher started up, its hydraulic hammers rhythmically smashing down on the fist-sized rocks, reducing them to pebbles.

"I'm not in a hurry," Morwen said. "I could give you a month or so to think about it." She picked up the projac and tucked it away. "Although, maybe by then, Belloch finds out where you are."

The pirate spoke now, a single word, not complimentary to Morwen Sabine.

"Fine," she said, rising to her feet. "I'll call the guards."

But when she turned toward the door, he said, "Wait."

She waited.

"How can you get me out?"

"Hipple didn't tell you about the maunch extract?"

By the way the man's brow congealed, she knew Hipple hadn't told them much. She said, "I work for Jerz Thanda. He sells extract to dealers on a dozen worlds in the Oikumene. He has his own fleet of space ships. I'm his right hand."

"Hipple told us you were a cook," the convict said.

"I was, for a while. Now I'm a drug smuggler."

He stared at the tabletop. She watched him process the new information. Then he looked up and said, "What do you want from me?"

"Information."

"About Belloch? You worked for him."

"I cooked for him. I need to know about his operation. About his alliances."

"Why?"

"That's my business."

She went alone to the Fifthday dance, interested to discover how many invitations out onto the floor she would receive, now that she was one of Thanda's complement. The experiment did not work, however. Eldo Kronik was already there, and Morwen was scarcely in the door before he hoved up before her and extended a hand. She let him wait a long moment before accepting it. She was coming to like the man, but her experience with Bod Hipple had made her aware that she lacked familiarity in relationships between men and women and the pitfalls they laid before the inexperienced.

Among the Dispers, dancing was a formal affair, with prescribed steps, bows and curtsies, promenades in line, and twirls while briskly clapping. Still, there were moments of relative tranquility during which words could be exchanged.

As they came to one of these periods, Morwen said, "Bod Hipple."

"Gone away," said Kronik.

"I know. But where?"

"Ask your boss."

The music accelerated and separated them. When next they came together, she said, "I did. He doesn't know."

Her answer drew a thoughtful look across Kronik's face as he twirled and clapped vigorously. Then each had to promenade at a distance too wide for private conversation. They came back into each other's orbit for a mutual arms-locked spin, and he said, "I warned him off after the business with Hubbley. He was jealous and impulsive, a bad combination."

The music skirled again and she said, "Let us talk outside."

Out in the cool evening air, she said, "He went to work for Thanda, maintaining the yacht's systems. But it wasn't a good fit."

"I can imagine," Kronik said.

"Then, one day, he didn't turn up for his shift. No one has seen him since."

The scrutineer's mouth quirked. "Hmm."

"Plus, he had been to Interchange."

"True," Kronik said. The wrinkles in his brow deepened.

"Now it turns out," Morwen said, "that he was waiting for my kidnappers at the Brumble's Corners. In their space ship, which left Providence while you were dealing with them."

"We knew he sicced them on you. For the reward, and for revenge." Kronik added an anatomical term that expressed a poor opinion of Bod Hipple's character.

They were both quiet for a while, each pursuing a new line of thought. Morwen broke the silence first.

"He knows a great deal about this place. Its defenses, its wealth, its physical layout." She paused, then caught his eye. "Its history."

Kronik turned to look up at the lights atop the hill. Three space ships were visible. "And Hacheem Belloch deals in slaves, cargoes, and ships."

"We need to talk to Thanda," Morwen said.

"Yes, we do. And soon." He reached for her hand. "But not before another dance."

Thanda came down to the constabulary, to meet with Morwen and Kronik. When the door was closed behind him, he said, "She says it's urgent. I've a lot to do, organizing shipments. Production is up three-fold since the spring."

Kronik said, "Exactly, how much are your shipments worth, these days?"

Thanda's face closed and he sent a glare Morwen's way. "None of your affair."

"Hear him out," Morwen said.

Thanda folded his arms. "Make it fast."

"I'll make it comprehensive," Kronik said. "We think Bod Hipple has gone to work for Hacheem Belloch. He's providing that pirate with the intelligence he would need to replay the Demon Princes' raid, only this time there will be ships and cargoes to be seized, as well as people."

Thanda's first take, evident on his face, was that the idea was far-fetched. "I have heavy weapons," he said. "Ison cannons. Disorganizers."

"Yes," said Morwen, "but who sold you those weapons? And where did you find people who know how to use them?"

That stopped her employer. After some thought, his arms left off their grip on each other and he said, "The crews were vetted."

"By whom? Who in your original complement of Protectors was qualified to judge origins and capabilities?"

Thanda took a deep breath, let it out. "Where is this coming from?" he said.

Between them, Morwen and Kronik laid out what they had learned and where they had learned it. When she told about Hipple waiting with the space ship at the crossroads hotel, his face darkened. When she told him what the rock-breaker had said, his face went pale.

"Right," he said when she was finished, "we need to double-vet every new hire. We need to see some test-fires of the weapons."

Kronik said, "The tests won't stir any suspicion. The vetting has to be done carefully."

"How do we do that?"

"You're not going to like it," the scrutineer said.

Thanda folded his arms again. "I haven't liked anything since I walked in here. Blaze away."

"Who has the best criminal information system in the Oikumene?" Kronik said.

Thanda swore, looked from one to the other, then said, "Really? The Ipsys?"

"You want information," Kronik said, "you go where the information is."

The Itinerator III was now the smallest of Thanda's fleet of five space ships. Morwen knew enough to engage the systems that let the ship fly itself. She and Kronik traveled to the Rigel Concourse — a slew of worlds long ago put into orbit around the great blue-white star by a vanished alien race whose motives had disappeared with them. They put down at the Avente Interplanetary Spaceport on Alphanor, capital of the Concourse worlds.

The ship's transponder had been altered to identify itself as a vessel from the nearby world of Diogenes. As the ship's drive shut down, port officials arrived to question the pair and inspect them for diseases and the vessel for contraband. Kronik advised them that they were police officers come to consult with the IPCC. Morwen tried to look the part in a uniform borrowed from Scrutineer Toba, though it was a little short in the cuffs. Kronik showed them his sigil and badge, and the inspection became perfunctory. The inspectors asked if he wanted the ship carried by the mobile crane into storage, and he demurred, saying they expected to be on-world only briefly.

Morwen and Kronik rode a hire-car to the Grand Esplanade overlooking the dark waters of the Thaumaturge Ocean, then turned into a wide avenue and proceeded a few streets more to a tall, cubical building occupying an entire block. Above the entrance, in large metallic letters, a sign read, *Interplanetary Police Coordinating Company*, with underneath a smaller line, *Rigel Concourse Headquarters*.

The lobby was fortified, the reception area ringed by walls of a transparent material designed to withstand weapons and explosives. A man in a buff and black uniform stood behind one barrier. His voice came over a speaker as he inquired as to their business.

Kronik spoke for both. "We are police agents from the community of New Dispensation on the world Providence. We wish to discuss affiliation with the IPCC."

The guard's expression did not change. He spoke into a hand-held device, words they could not hear, then he directed them toward a booth behind the barriers at one side of the reception area.

"Enter that, one at a time, and do as directed."

Kronik went first. The booth's scanners determined that he possessed no weapons or implants. A door opposite the one by which he had entered slid aside, and he stepped out into a room with chairs. He waited for Morwen to join him and they both sat.

After a brief time, a door opened and a middle-aged woman in a uniform similar to the guard's beckoned them to follow. They progressed along corridors and rose in an ascensor until they were led to an office with a window that looked out on the street, with the Esplanade and the ocean at its end. The room contained a desk, two chairs, and a lean, efficient-looking man whose name plate said he was Colonel-Inspector Ben Zaum. He bade them sit and took up a stylus with a practiced manner.

"You wish affiliation with the IPCC?" he asked.

"No," said Morwen. "We said that only to gain admission."

The agent's hand went to a panel to one side of his desk. He pressed a button. Then he said, "You will have a few seconds before armed officers appear. If you have something to say, this is your opportunity."

Morwen said, "We come from a world in the Beyond. We expect to be raided by the notorious pirate, Hacheem Belloch —"

She got no further before three serious-looking IPCC officers, two male and one female, entered the room and spread themselves to give optimum lines of fire. Each pointed a projac at the seated pair. Both Morwen and Kronik sat very still.

The man behind the desk raised a hand to tell the agents to wait. "Go on," he said.

"We assume that you have more information about Belloch than we do," Morwen said. "We hope you will provide us with some of that information."

Zaum's brows raised themselves. "Why would we do that?"

Kronik spoke, "Because we will coordinate our response to the raid. Specifically, we will let you know when the incursion is to happen, so that you may swoop in and take Belloch and his pirates into IPCC custody."

Zaum touched another button on his console. A screen appeared in the air before him and he entered a few strokes on a keyboard. The pair from Providence could not see what he was seeing, but the information became clear when he looked at them and said, "New Dispensation. Source of the maunch extract trade."

"That is true," said Kronik. "The substance is legal on many worlds in the Oikumene."

"And illegal on some others," Zaum said.

Kronik shrugged. "I assume the IPCC, like any other police organization, recognizes a scale of villainy. Maunch extract outrages the followers of some political philosophies. Hacheem Belloch murders, enslaves, and steals, then runs back to the Beyond. His compound on Blatcher's World is a fortress. An assault there would cost scores of lives, perhaps hundreds."

Morwen put in, "But catch him away from his hidey-hide, with only light weapons…"

Zaum regarded them, his thoughts unshown on his face. Then he turned to the three armed agents. "Dismissed."

They holstered their weapons and turned to leave. Zaum said to them, "You didn't hear any of that."

Ben Zaum took them to the basement, to a large well lit room in which more than a score of men and women worked at consoles, consulted screens, wrote or dictated reports, or leafed through heavy tomes so large they required their own custom-made stands.

Zaum approached a woman with age-grayed hair tied in a bun on the top of her head and a stylus tucked behind one ear. He said, "Gela, I need the file on associates of Hacheem Belloch."

She did not ask why, but put aside the file she had been reading, rose from her desk, and went to a wall full of shelves and pigeon holes. Here she ran a finger along one level until she stopped at a fat folder of brown card-stock wrapped in a red ribbon. She pulled it loose and took it to a stand-up viewing counter, where she unwound the ribbon and opened the file.

"Images of known associates," Zaum said. Then to Morwen, "Show her."

Morwen produced the several photographs of Jerz Thanda's recent hires, each taken for the Protector's identification plaque. She handed them over to Gela, who glanced at the first photo, discarded it on the counter top, and went on to the next image beneath.

Over the next minute, she sorted through thirty images, placing them in two piles on the counter: one numbering twenty-seven, the other only three. When she had finished, she leafed through the folder and found three files. These she spread on the counter top, then placed one of the three images on each.

Kronik and Morwen leaned forward. There was no question that the three Protectors matched the faces in the files, though the names did not. They read the details of each man's known criminal activities and the instructions to detain on sight and to be aware that these persons were armed and dangerous.

"That one," Morwen said, tapping a photo, "is head of the crew that serves the ison cannon. This one," another tap, "is one of the perimeter guards."

Gela spoke now. "Belloch does not pick his targets randomly. He has a network of scouts who identify possibilities and report back to him. These three are some of his most trusted agents. If they are embedded somewhere, it is somewhere he is definitely interested in."

"Thank you," Kronik said. He indicated the three files. "May we have copies?"

Gela made a small sound of discomfort. Zaum said, "After redactions. Some of the information in there could lead to exposure of our sources."

"Your weasels," Kronik said.

"We prefer to call them sources."

"Redact away," Kronik said. "We are grateful for this."

Zaum gestured to the door. "Let us return to my office and discuss how we remain in touch."

But as they turned to leave, Gela said, "Let me look again at those images."

She sorted through them again, arriving at one of the twenty-seven she had at first discarded. "Is it only Belloch's KAs you are interested in?" she said.

Kronik and Morwen exchanged a look. "Not necessarily," Morwen said.

Gela set the photo on the counter and crossed to the wall of shelves again, sought and found another file, and brought it back to the counter. She leafed through this one until she found what she was searching for. "Ah," she said, and drew out a file with an image that matched that of the Protector she had singled out.

She scanned the document, then said, "I thought I recognized him. He's not an associate of Belloch, but he is always a person of interest."

She showed the file to Morwen and Kronik. They read it with interest that soon grew into alarm.

Morwen read aloud the notation high up on the page: "Underchief in the corsair company of Sheleen Two Hearts."

Zaum looked at the face of the guard who had stopped Morwen the first time she ventured up Mount Pleasant to meet Jerz Thanda.

"Now," the IPCC man said, "I'm even more interested in your raid."

Morwen produced another image from her pocket. She showed it

Barbarians of the Beyond

to Gela and Zaum. "Have you any information about this man's where-abouts?"

Gela shook her head and said. "Is he one of Belloch's?"

"He may be. A recent hire."

Zaum took the photo. "We do not have agents inside his establishment, but we have some close by. We will see if they know him. Does he have a name?"

Morwen said, "Yes. Bod Hipple."

"Is he important?" Zaum said.

Kronik answered, "We think he may be the thread we can pull to unravel the whole plot."

"Then we'll let you know," Zaum said. "Come up to my office and we will discuss details of how to remain in touch."

He accompanied Morwen and Kronik to the door. In the corridor, Zaum said, "What do you know of Malagate the Woe?"

Kronik answered. "What everybody knows. A Star King. He was part of the Demon Princes' raid that removed the original population of our community. He is in charge of collecting tribute from the settlements on Providence, including from the Protectors of New Dispensation."

None of this appeared to be news to Zaum. "What have you heard lately?"

Kronik thought for a moment. "Nothing," he said. "Come to think of it, I have not seen his collector overflying our town in an air car in a couple of months. And he used to be as regular as the sunrise."

The Ipsy nodded. "Absence of evidence is sometimes evidence of absence. Perhaps you would let us know if his collector returns."

"We can do," said Kronik. "What's on your mind?"

"We keep a watchful eye on the Demon Princes, as best we can," said Zaum. "Lately, that eye has not been able to fall upon Attel Malagate, not since he dropped in to Smade's Tavern on Smade's Planet, some months back."

Morwen said, "Meaning he is holed up somewhere, plotting another dastardly extravaganza?"

Zaum's hand moved in an equivocal gesture. "Perhaps. Or perhaps he has been killed."

Kronik blew out a wordless puff of air. "That would be quite an

— 131 —

accomplishment. I would be interested in meeting whoever pulled that off."

"As would I," said Ben Zaum.

Back in the Colonel-Investigator's office, they discussed the details of who would bring the two from Providence the information they needed, where and when the transfer would take place. But when they left IPCC headquarters, their business in Avente was finished. Zaum offered them a car to take them back to the spaceport, but Kronik declined.

"It would be a shame to have traversed the Grand Esplanade in both directions without having at least sampled its attractions."

So they walked down to the great promenade and sauntered along it for a while, the dark ocean to their right displaying a road of molten light running out to where Rigel was dipping toward the horizon. Eastward, three planets of the Concourse hung in the evening sky like lanterns.

"Which worlds are they?" Morwen wondered.

"I think that on the left is Krokinole," Kronik said, "by its redness. But as for the others, I couldn't say. Tantamount, my home world, must be on the other side of Rigel."

About them, the folk of Avente moved in leisurely manners. No one hurried on the Esplanade; they sauntered, perambulated, sashayed, all in their fashionable attire, the skin of their faces and hands tinted in the latest colors, seeing and being seen. Morwen and Kronik, clearly offworlders, drew some small interest for their untinted faces and off-world uniforms, but glances that came their way did not linger.

They came to a set of steps that led up to a restaurant with outdoor tables, where diners could watch the crowds and experience whatever sublime emotions the imperturbable ocean might raise up in them. Thanda had fortified them with a bundle of high-denomination svu certificates — "in case you need to sweeten some official" — and Kronik proposed they take a memorable meal on the maunch industry's ducats.

They sat on the terrace and regarded the crowd swirling slowly along, beneath the great star's stately progress toward the horizon. A server brought them the first course from the set menu: diminutive pastries containing steamed crustaceans from the ocean, bathed in a variety of sauces, piquant, creamy, something like a pesto, another that reminded Morwen of fennel, but not as sweet.

"You could cook like this," Kronik said as he reached to refill their glasses of pale, effervescent wine from the carafe.

"I couldn't get the sea creatures," she answered. "And some of the seasonings are new to me."

"I meant, you could come to a place like this and earn a living."

"Live in the Oikumene?" she said. "It took me all my life to get to Providence, and you think I should leave?"

"Your goal was to bring your parents home, and you've done that. Now you are free to make your own choices."

She regarded him over the rim of her wine glass. "And one of those choices, would it involve you?"

He met her stare. "It could." He looked out over the sea, then turned back to her. "I have always been impressed by the IPCC. Most of the policing I've done in New Diss has been sobering up drunks on Fifthday night and looking for weasels, though I don't think the two that we delivered to Thanda were anything but just wanderers passing through."

"And did they wander on?" she said.

"No, and I regret that," he said. "But back to what I started to say: our visit today reminded me what police work at a higher level looks like. I found it...attractive."

And you find me attractive, was her unvoiced reply. Aloud, she said, "What about the community? Your obligation to your fellow Dispers? Your oath?"

He shrugged. "I have largely been displaced by Thanda. At first that concerned me, but he has been a sensible and forward-thinking leader, rare enough in the Beyond. I believe he understands that a happy populace makes for a successful enterprise."

"Well," said Morwen, and left it at that, letting him see that she was thinking about what he was telling her.

"But, of course," Kronik said, "we have a couple of pirates to deal with."

"And a jilted lover bent on revenge," she said. "You would not be of that sort, would you?"

"Never," he said, pouring them more wine. "Bereft of your affections, I would merely dwindle and expire."

"I should hope so," she said. She extended her glass and they touched rims. Then she voiced a thought that had been occurring to her lately.

"You know everything about me, down to the constituents of my gene plasm. Of you, I know only what I have seen."

"You want the whole story, or just the important bits?"

"We'll start with the important bits, then see where they lead."

He took another sip of wine, set down the glass, and ran a thoughtful finger around the rim. "It's a funny story," he said. "I was a junior provost on Tantamount. I met this young woman, and there was a spark. Then she fell in with the Prophet's movement, began to chew the maunch. Like many a new convert, she became an enthusiast, wanting to enlist everyone in her circle."

He took another sip of wine. "I did not care very much, one way or another, but to please her, I began coming to the meet-ups. Finally, I took the sacrament. It had a good effect on me. I also liked the sense of community, which had been lacking in my life.

"But then the frictions with those outside the community began to build up. The Prophet began to talk about going out beyond the Pale to find a new world. He had already heard about the town standing empty on Providence and was steering the faithful toward an exodus.

"He knew about my being a provostsman and offered me the job of organizing and training a town constabulary. It sounded interesting so I signed on.

"Then came the day of departure. I waited at the spaceport for my intended to arrive. Instead, there was a message on my communicator. She was not coming, had changed her mind about leaving Tantamount. She invited me to stay, too."

Morwen said, "She was the changeable type."

"That she was," said Kronik. "It occurred to me that there would almost certainly be further changes down the road, just as sudden and just as drastic. I boarded the ship and left Tantamount behind."

Morwen poured him some more wine. "That was definitely an 'important bit.' I'm still waiting for the funny part."

"I suppose it depends on your definition of 'funny'." He gestured to her with the glass and drained half of its contents.

They ate in silence for a while, then she said, "These people —" a wave of her hand took in the pedestrians and the diners at other tables "— they think of us Beyonders as barbarians, do they not?"

"If they think of us at all," he said. Then, realizing that she was serious, "To them, I suppose we *are* barbarous. We see things, some of us do things, that they encounter only in stories and entertainments."

She lifted the last tart. "You lived among them, raised on a 'civilized' world. Could we be like them? Would they let us, if they knew what we have seen and done?"

She popped a pastry into her mouth. He accepted her questions as rhetorical. He did not raise the prospect of life in the Oikumene again.

Back in New Dispensation, they told Jerz Thanda what they had learned. His face went cold at the news of the four infiltrators, though his eyes seemed to show a dark light.

Kronik said, "We can't take them right away. We first need to know when the raid will come. They may be in touch with their patrons, and if the four of them suddenly disappear from Belloch's and Two Hearts's view, they will be warned off."

"Would that not be a good thing?" Thanda said.

Morwen said, "Only if it meant they had given up on the idea. But there is so much here to be taken — ships, souls, bundles of SVU certificates — the temptation will always exist. And therefore the threat."

Thanda agreed. "Then let us make a plan."

A shipment of extract was scheduled for Olliphane, one of the Concourse worlds where maunch extract was prohibited. Morwen went along as a supernumerary. As the pilot turned off the intersplit drive, he also disabled the vessel's transponder. They slipped into the atmosphere and descended to a clearing in a forest zone on the planet's nightside, far removed from the pools of light that denoted civilization. Three air cars, carryalls with extended luggage compartments, waited beneath camouflage nets.

The off-loading was practiced and swift. Men appeared from the trees to form hand-to-hand chains that transferred packages of the extract to the air cars. As each vehicle's space was filled, it lifted off and flew without running lights at treetop height. When the last of the extract was gone, Thanda's pilot said, "We cannot stay long."

"Wait," Morwen said, and they did.

A short time after, another air car appeared, unmarked by any insignia and also without running lights. It set down into the clearing and its canopy went up. Morwen approached.

The man in the operator's seat, a dark shape only, said, "Not yet. Next venue." The vehicle silently rose and sped away.

The "next venue" came several days later. This time Morwen went to Pilgham, a world where maunch extract was legal, though its distribution was regulated by the health care system. Thanda's ship touched down at a spaceport on the southern continent. Officials came on board with documents and stamps, the packages were opened and samples tested for purity. The process was performed at an unhurried pace.

While this was happening, Morwen went to the port's transient section and had found a pub called The Comet's Tail. She sat at the bar and ordered a mug of ale and some crispy chitons, and glanced through a periodical left there by a customer who departed as she came in.

Between the publication's pages was a slip of paper. She palmed it and continued reading. When the ale was finished, she picked her teeth to dislodge fragments of chitons and returned to the ship. Not long after, the officials departed with the cargo, and they headed back to Providence.

She sat with Kronik and Thanda behind closed doors in the constabulary. The piece of paper lay before them on the desk. Kronik brought out the map of Belloch's estate that Zaum had given them. The pirate's fortified compound lay outside the town of Boregore on the Big Island in the Maidan Archipelago on Blatcher's World. The main streets of the town were marked, as well as some of the minor avenues.

"There it is," Kronik said, pointing to a small street near the center of Boregore.

Morwen leaned in. "I know that place," she said. "I used to be sent on errands into the town. It's a lodging house for people who come and go, sailors and the like, who aren't important enough to be invited into the compound."

She paused to think. "Or for people Belloch doesn't want to be seen with. He knows there are weasels watching his comings and goings."

"Would the IPCC have anybody within the compound?" Thanda said.

Morwen signaled a negative. "The least suspicion, and you find your fingers being burned off, one at a time."

"So," said Kronik, "do we snatch him? If so, how?"

"The how is easy," Morwen said. "The house provides no food. There's a restaurant here," she tapped one side of the square, then indicated another spot, "and a tavern here. He must spend some of his evenings in those places. We could catch him on the way home. There's an alley two doors from his lodgings."

"Then what?" said Kronik. "We can't let him go."

Morwen was thinking. "We'd need a cart, just a handcart would do. And we would not let him go."

"If he disappeared," Thanda said, "that might alert Belloch. They may even think he was a weasel."

"He would not disappear," said Morwen. When they looked at her, she said, "That's a dangerous neighborhood."

Morwen and Kronik spent two days roughening their hands and allowing a sun lamp to redden their faces. Then, again with Thanda's most trusted pilot, Lech Macrine, they set off for Blatcher's World, deep in the Beyond. When they arrived, there were no formalities to endure. They came down at a spaceport on Golden Land — which had never lived up to its name — and reenergized the drives. Then they lifted off and flew within the atmosphere across the Sibilant Sea toward the Maidan Archipelago.

As they approached the chain of islands, Macrine took them down to wave-top height and they traveled on for another hour. Then he deployed the inflatable landers and they settled gently onto the water. Morwen and Kronik opened the main hatch and pushed the battered, four-person lifeboat out onto the sea. They loaded in a few supplies, then boarded.

The pilot took the space ship aloft, but only just, and flew back the way they had come. Kronik broke out the oars. "We'll take turns," he said. He looked up at Blatcher's Star, hot and yellow at the zenith, and said, "We can deepen our sunburns."

Near sunset, with Morwen at the oars, they came laboriously into the harbor at Boregore. Several idlers, some of them moderately drunk, watched them from the landing. When she and Kronik, their faces peeling and their shoulders stooped from fatigue, climbed the ladder one of them stepped forward and helped them take the final step.

"Watch your boat?" he said, around a belch of fumes that said he had been drinking Blue Ruin.

"Keep it," said Kronik. He peered inland and saw a tavern. "They got beds in there?"

"Ahuh," said the idler.

Shortly after, Kronik and Morwen occupied a small room with two bunks, one above the other. She climbed to the top and stretched out. "That was harder than I thought," she said. "That offshore current."

Kronik's answer was a snore.

They spent two days scouting and preparing. The alley they had seen on the map was as useful as Morwen remembered. A two-wheeled fishmonger's cart, used to haul catches from the harbor to his shop, stood outside the rear door of his establishment, its reek guaranteeing it remained unmolested. Kronik went to three different chandlers and bought what he needed: a short length of flexible hose, a lead fishing weight, some copper wire, and a roll of all-purpose tape. From these he assembled a rudimentary instrument that he and his constables would have called a "pacifier," the kind of head-cracker that would be wielded by a criminal of the lowest rank. He also acquired some implements that comprised a basic torture kit.

Morwen kept to their room, Kronik telling the tavern's proprietor, who cared only that the rent be paid, that his wife was exhausted by the ordeal of rowing from their sunken catamaran, wrecked on a reef. She only came out to use the outdoor jakes, and kept her face averted and her tattooed arm covered. It was unlikely that anyone would know her on sight, but the tattoo was money to be had.

When Kronik had assembled everything he needed, and found, at the end of the alley, a quiet and secluded place to conduct the interrogation, they approached the town square in the evening and saw Bod Hipple descend from his lodgings and cross to the restaurant. Not long after, he left the restaurant, picking his teeth, and went into the tavern.

"Let us be ready," Morwen said.

They went down the alley to the fishmonger's and wheeled his cart to near the mouth of the passageway. Then they watched and waited.

People came and went in the square, though none lingered. They could hear conversations and the clink of tableware and crockery from the restaurant, and outbursts of raucous singing from the tavern. At one point, two men came out of the latter, cursing and shoving each other. They attempted a fistfight, but were too far soaked in drink to make much progress. Eventually, they put their arms around each other's shoulders and staggered off in renewed bonhomie.

Late in the evening, Bod Hipple emerged onto the square and listed toward the rooming house. His uneven gait made Kronik whisper, "Eight pints, at least."

They had planned the maneuver. As Hipple made to pass the mouth of the alley, Morwen stepped out into the light and blocked his path.

"Bod," she said. "Is that you?"

The man's mouth fell comically open. At that moment, Eldo Kronik came up behind him and applied the pacifier to the back of Hipple's skull. His knees buckled and the two attackers caught him before he could fall. Moments later, he was sprawled face-down among the fish scales, and Kronik was wheeling the cart deeper into the alley. He stopped where the passageway ended at a blank wall. One window overlooked the place, but it was unlit.

Now they wrapped Hipple's wrists, knees, and ankles with the leftover tape and laid a strip across his mouth.

"Careful he doesn't vomit," Kronik said. "We don't want him choking to death."

He squatted on his heels and felt the bump on the back of Hipple's head. "Not too bad," he said. "He'll come to in a bit."

"Fine," said Morwen. She could see Kronik studying her in the dim light. "What?" she said.

He looked away, toward the mouth of the alley. "Take the cart back to where we left it and keep watch."

"What? Why? No."

"We didn't discuss this," he said. "What I'm about to do will not be pleasant viewing."

She gave a short laugh that had only the darkest humor in it, and squatted beside him. "Not far from here," she said, "I was compelled to watch people whipped at Hacheem Belloch's orders. Sometimes, the whipmen worked in pairs, spelling each off when they tired, and keeping on until the poor wretch was dead."

Kronik started to say something, but she put her fingers to his lips. "It takes a lot of whipping to kill a grown man or woman. And this *fagreen*—" she used a word that described a noxious reptiloid native to Blatcher's World "—will cause my parents to be strung up in front of me and whipped to death. Then it will be my turn."

She looked up the alley. "I'll move the cart because it will block the view of what we are doing. But then I'll be back."

Kronik knew how to deal with recalcitrant suspects. The Deweaseling Corps had taught him that the application of pain in the context of helplessness, coupled with the expectation of worse to come, was a useful technique employed by local police in the Beyond. Even had Bod Hipple tried to be brave and remain true to the pirate who had bought him, Kronik would have cracked his resolve. As it was, his courage evaporated faster than morning dew on a summer day.

"Good of you to cooperate," Kronik said, when he was sure they had the information they needed. "In return, I'll make this quick and painless."

Hipple had something to say to that but the words never came. Kronik pressed his thumbs against two spots on the man's throat. Hipple instantly lost consciousness, his head lolling forward onto his chest. The scrutineer then pinched the unconscious man's nostrils shut and pressed his lips together. He held them thus until the lower structures of Hipple's brain recognized a need for air.

The man jerked as his diaphragm tried to make his lungs fill. But the pathways for the needed oxygen were blocked. The attempt to regain consciousness failed and Hipple slumped again. Kronik continued the pressure for a while, then put two fingers to the man's neck.

"Gone," he said.

"Good," said Morwen. She thought to say the death was easier than he deserved, but she saw that Kronik was dealing with his own emotions and left the thought unvoiced.

They removed the tape from his wrists and ankles, turned his pockets inside out, and took a wad of svu certificates out of his wallet. They dragged his body nearer to the mouth of the alley and left him there. Kronik dropped the pacifier beside the corpse. The picture would be clear when he was found in the morning: he had come drunk out of the tavern, been followed by someone who worked on the fish boats or in the drying sheds — the scales from the cart would be the clue — then struck on the head. The minor bruises from Kronik's expert torture would look like ordinary wear and tear.

Hacheem Belloch might have his suspicions, but the evidence should serve to quell them.

Morwen and Kronik returned the cart to the fishmonger's then went back to their lodgings. Their room was loud with the raucous goings-on in the tavern below, but Morwen climbed up to her bunk and lay with her hands folded on her belly. The memory of Hipple's useless pleas came to her, but she had seen much worse inflicted on people she cared about. She overlaid those impressions with memories of Belloch's punishments. When they returned to the Manse overlooking New Dispensation, she would have to do worse things to the infiltrators. She formed images in her mind and let them linger. The images were unpleasant, but she had seen worse.

Soon after, she slept.

Two days later, she and Kronik got tickets on a jitney that crossed the Big Island and connected with a ferry that steamed to the islets of the Salamanders Group. In the evening, they walked an hour to a secluded cove. Near midnight a small light showed itself three times, out to sea. Kronik produced a lumen and flashed it twice, paused, then twice again.

Thanda's space ship came silently toward them, putting down on its floats near the water's edge. Morwen and Kronik waded out and climbed aboard.

Chapter Eight

"I have to tell them something," Morwen said to Thanda. "When the ships come down, they will be terrified. They may try to kill themselves. That was their intent if my rescue plan failed."

"No one can know anything," Thanda said. "The merest hint that we know what's coming…" He spread his hands.

"Could I take them offworld? A vacation?"

"No variation in routines," Thanda said. "We're assuming the infiltrators are providing intelligence to their chiefs. If we show any sudden changes to normal practice, Belloch and Two Hearts could change their plans. They could reschedule for another date, and then they might catch us only half-prepared."

Kronik and Morwen had come back from Blatcher's World knowing the date of the coming raid. They had suspected that Bod Hipple would have advised the pirates to descend on the town on Founder's Day, a holiday when the whole population of New Dispensation gathered at the meeting house to celebrate the arrival of the pioneers led by the Prophet Armbruch. Most of the adults would take the sacrament. They would be easy prey for the sudden onslaught.

They had been right about the date and about Hipple's advocacy for it. He had been looking forward to accompanying his new employer.

Between now and then, no disruption of routine among the Protectors would occur. No one, outside of Morwen, Thanda, and Kronik knew the date or that an attack was coming. Macrine the pilot had been sworn to secrecy, with the promise of reward and the threat of death if he mentioned the trip to Blatcher's World.

On the morning of the raid, Thanda would order a weapons drill.

As the Protectors deployed, he would send his most trusted men — the ones who had been with him since the beginning — to arrest Belloch's and Two Hearts's four plants, and kill them if they resisted.

"They mean to surprise us," Thanda said. "We have to surprise them."

Chaffe and Elva Sabine were adapting to their new lives. Working conditions in Thanda's kitchens were good. When they had asked for additional equipment and materials, their wishes had been gratified. Their quarters were private and comfortable. They had begun to make, if not friends, then friendly acquaintances among the Dispers. Even some of the Protectors were well disposed to them: the ones who knew good cooking from mediocre and appreciated the perquisite.

Her parents had lost some of their hunted and haunted look. The stiffness of longstanding fear lingered in their postures but it had begun to ease. They smiled more, even laughed at times.

Morwen had encouraged them to come to meet-ups and had convinced them, after several sessions, to chew the maunch. She had been afraid the psychedelic might call up demons from their lower minds; it had that effect on some, which was why the extract was banned on worlds like Krokinole. But Chaffe and Elva experienced the beatific effects and came down from the stage smiling. Their walk back to the Manse was long, because they kept stopping to exclaim over the sight of some mundane detail of the town that now took on an aura of meaning.

After her meeting with Thanda, Morwen went down to the kitchens, finding her parents preparing the noon meal. They greeted her with hugs and kisses on her cheeks. She took up a knife and began cutting up peeled krava roots, tossing the yellow rounds into a great steel pot boiling on the range.

"Are you going to mash these?" she asked.

"No," said her father, "boil them to soften the fibers then roast them in drippings from last night's legs of shumkin."

Morwen kept at the chopping until all of the krava were simmering in the hot water. She set down the knife and stared at the wall.

Her mother had stopped shredding lettuce and was watching her. "What's the matter?" Elva said.

"Nothing," Morwen said. "I'm fine."

"Is it to do with Eldo? Boy trouble?"

Morwen couldn't quite suppress a laugh. "No, no boy trouble."

"Then what?"

Morwen put on a smile. "Just something to do with the job. But it will all work out soon. Everything is going to be fine. Just remember that."

Her father said, "I like that Kronik, even if he's wound a little tight."

"He'll be happy to hear that," Morwen said.

"What does he like to eat?" Elva said. "We could have him up for a meal, just the four of us."

"I'll ask him."

"You ought to know by now," her mother said. "That and a lot more about him."

"Mother…" Morwen began, then recognized the wisdom of retreat in the face of overwhelming force. "I've got to get back to work."

Founder's Day dawned warm and clear, the skies empty of clouds except for a few piled up on the southern horizon. After breakfast, the streets began to fill with Dispers, walking in family groups toward the meeting house. There was a holiday mood, people laughing, children running and skipping, many carrying colored balloons on sticks that would later be used in the mock battles that commemorated the struggles between Dispers and their former neighbors on the world Tantamount, where the Society of the New Dispensation began.

From up at the Manse, Morwen watched the crowds gathering then went to eat a late breakfast in the cafeteria. Most of the dayshift Protectors were finishing their meals, keeping an eye on the chronometer as it edged toward starting time. She seated herself at the table where Thanda's "originals" tended to gather. She spoke quietly to two of them. After a while, they drained their mugs of punge and left.

Morwen glanced over to where two of Belloch's plants were eating at the same table as Two Hearts's man, the three-striper who had challenged her when she first came to see Thanda. Did they seem tense? Did they show any signs of anticipation? She couldn't be sure.

She picked at her food, too wound up to eat. The images of what she meant to do kept rising on her mind's inner screen, but she made no effort to dispel them. Finally, she drained her mug of punge and rose. The infiltrators were also up and moving toward the door. And there in the doorway was the fourth operative, coming off the overnight shift. She saw nods and looks and it was plain: *Today is the day.*

Hipple had said that the plan was for one of the plants to send a signal when the Dispers were all at the meeting house. Four ships would come down: one at the Manse and the other three to block the main roads to east, west, and south. Assault teams would pour out of the vessels, form a perimeter, and move inward toward the meeting house. Resistance, expected from the Manse and the constabulary, would be suppressed by firepower, while the Manse's heavy weapons, under the control of secret pirates, would fail to respond.

It was much the same as what she knew of the Demon Princes' raid on Mount Pleasant, from what Morwen's parents had told her when she was young. Indeed, she wouldn't be surprised if either or both of Belloch and Two Hearts, younger and full of ambition in those days, had been part of the attack that had captured her parents.

She went to Thanda's office. He was meeting with his picked originals, including the two Morwen had spoken to in the cafeteria, informing them of the impending attack. Issuing the men with projacs, he named the four infiltrators, exposed their plan, and told his men that it would be useful but not necessary to take three of them alive, but the man in charge of the disorganizer crew would have a communicator. They needed to know what message he would transmit.

Morwen watched with Thanda from his window that overlooked the courtyard where Protectors assembled for pre-shift parades. The senior Protector, Subcommander Gwllero, stood on a box and made routine announcements regarding the day's work. Then he told the ranks of men that there would be a heavy weapons drill at midmorning.

The infiltrators were grouped together in the second rank. Morwen saw them exchange glances, but the message-sender gave a slight negative shake of his head. Then Gwllero shouted, "Parade, dismissed!" and the massed stomping down of scores of boots signaled the end of the event.

The four plants broke away from the mass of Protectors. They would have split up then and gone to their various assignments, the nightshifter probably heading for bed for an hour or so of sleep. But they were swiftly surrounded by armed men and marched toward a strongly built building that stored maunch extract and bundles of svu certificates brought back from other worlds.

A few of the other Protectors noticed, but Thanda's subcommander strode over and told them to get about their duties. A moment later, the four captives were out of sight.

Thanda crossed to a cupboard and withdrew a long-barreled disorganizer. "Do you have your projac?" he asked Morwen. When she produced the weapon, he said, "Let's go."

She noticed that her hand did not shake.

The four pirates were on their knees in the stronghouse, hands clasped behind their heads. The originals were spread around them, projacs aimed. Morwen and Thanda entered and walked to where the prisoners could see them.

Morwen asked one of the Protectors, "Did you find the communicator?"

For answer, he showed her a small device.

"Which one had it?"

The Protector indicated the man on the far right of the line of kneeling men. He was the three-striper, underchief to Sheleen Two Hearts.

Morwen faced him. She had steeled herself for this moment, as she had for the business with Bod Hipple. She thought of her parents, smiling and laughing at the meet-up. Then she thought of them hanging from Hacheem Belloch's hook, the iron-tipped whip curling about them, tearing away tender flesh.

She said to the man, "You are now going to die." He disdained to look at her. She continued, "You have a choice as to how. You can die like this —" she clenched her teeth, aimed her projac, and shot a beam of energy into the head of the man beside the pirate she was talking to. The victim's head became a glowing mass of flesh and bone, then the overheated brain burst the cranium. Fragments of hot bone and boiling flesh splattered against the face and neck of the pirate who was to give the signal for the raid to begin. The dead man toppled forward, steam rising from his shattered skull.

Two Hearts's man trembled, hot gore dripping from the side of his face, but he did not respond.

Morwen said, "Or you can die like this."

She nodded to Thanda who thumbed the disorganizer into humming life and aimed it at the next man in line. The pirate screamed and leapt to his feet, turned and ran toward the door. Thanda adjusted the disorganizer's aperture and raised the weapon to his shoulder, aiming it at the fleeing man's feet.

He depressed the stud and the disorganizer shrieked, its sparkling black energy leaping out in a narrow beam. It scorched the floorboards immediately behind the running pirate then touched the heel of one foot. The flesh began to dissolve. Morwen saw exposed bone, then it, too, liquefied into a thick, glutinous gunk, gray and pink. The effect crept forward as the man fell to his knees then rolled over onto his back. He grasped his calf with both hands, holding his leg in the air, watching in horror and agony as his foot was fully affected. The greasy liquid dripped onto his belly, raising smoke from the black cloth of his Protector's garb.

He let go of his leg and brushed at the smoldering spots. And now he began to scream.

The starmenter who was to give the signal had not turned to look. But he could not avoid hearing the screams. His face paled and his lips spasmed.

Despite all her mental preparations, Morwen was fighting to keep her breakfast from coming up. She didn't trust herself to utter a full sentence. "Well?"

"I'll tell you," the pirate said.

"Good." Morwen walked to where the screaming man lay and shot him through the head. She came up behind the other kneeling prisoner. He was mumbling something that might have been a prayer. She let him finish then killed him.

"Get him up and take him to my office," Thanda said. As he passed Morwen on the way out, he said, "I knew you were the one to hire."

"You will tell us the procedure," Thanda told the man taped into the chair. "We will then wait. You will do what you say you are supposed to do, then we will see what happens."

He gestured to the disorganizer, standing upright against the wall, near to his hand. "If the ships come down, as expected, you get a quick death. If you have played us false —" he touched the weapon lightly "— I will slowly disorganize you. It may take hours. Are we clear?"

"Clear," the pirate said. "There is no special code. I just tell them we're ready."

Thanda touched the disorganizer again, his face saying the gesture was a reminder.

"No special code," the starmenter said again.

They waited. Thanda called in Subcommander Gwllero, told him of the impending attack, and ordered him to prepare the Protectors to receive the assault. At Thanda's behest, Morwen called Kronik on her communicator and brought him up to date. He told her that his men were now informed of the threat and were heading for the meeting house. They would warn the people, send them down to the basement, and fortify the place as well as they could with furniture and other materials that could block doors and windows. The air car with the disorganizer would be placed on the roof, ready to take out any vehicles the attackers might bring up.

And then they waited some more. After what seemed several hours but was not, the pirate's communicator offered a low-volume *beep*.

Morwen picked it up, clicked its activator, and held it to the pirate's ear.

"Ready," he said.

There was a click as the connection was broken. Morwen took the device away. Thanda's eyes narrowed. "Ready?" he said. "That was all?"

"That was all. Watch the sky."

They waited, Thanda drumming his fingers on the desk. One of his Protectors was at the window with a macroscope. "There," he said, pointing north.

They all crowded in to take a look. At first, it looked like one dark dot, but as the space craft descended they split into four distinct objects, each growing larger as they fell out of the empty blue.

Thanda took the macroscope and adjusted its mechanism. "Those aren't ships of war. Three are cargo carriers, and one is a small passenger liner."

He reached for his own communicator and spoke into it, "All units. Enemy in sight. Wait for my orders. No one is to fire on the ships. Personnel and assault vehicles only. Repeat, no fire on the ships. And wait for the command."

He closed the communicator and spoke to Morwen. "Tell Kronik what's happening, and remind him of the fire plan."

Morwen did as instructed. Kronik's voice spoke in her ear. "Understood."

"Look after my parents," she said.

"They have been encouraged to take the sacrament," he said. "It has calmed them. Down in the basement, they will not know what is happening until it is over."

The ships landed virtually at the same moment. Hatches opened and disgorged men and vehicles: air cars, ground cars, cargo carriers of both kinds. Thanda observed from his window.

"No military vehicles," he said.

"We can't get them," the bound pirate said. He swallowed and said, "I'm ready now, if you want to do it."

"I've decided not to," Thanda said, with as impish a grin as his hard face could manage. "You're a member of Sheleen Two Hearts's key crew. That means you're worth 30,000 svu to the IPCC. I think I'll take the money."

He took a shocker from his desk and rendered the man senseless.

The pirates were taking their time getting organized, Morwen thought, watching from the window. The lack of action from the Manse must make them think their plan has succeeded.

"Here they come," she said.

"Yes," said Thanda. He spoke into his communicator. "All units, open fire, fire at will."

The Protectors had been called out for a weapons drill and were still at their posts, keeping out of sight but armed and with the heavy weapons already powered up. Their officers had told them of the pirates' plans to catch them unprepared, ripe for slaughter or captivity. The Protectors had waited, most of them concealed, as the passenger liner came down onto the upper landing pad above the Manse. Now, as the invaders formed into squads and rushed toward the various positions they had studied while en route to Providence, the defenders opened fire with projacs and projectile weapons.

It was a slaughter. The raiders went down in swathes, only a few of them living long enough to return ineffective fire. Those who were not killed or wounded by the first volley threw themselves down behind whatever cover they could find, or just prone upon the ground. But the weapons drill meant that the Protectors were so placed as to enjoy overlapping fields of fire. There was no cover to be had.

More than a hundred pirates had come out of the small liner that had landed above the Manse. In less than a minute there were no more than a dozen who were not lying dead or screaming from their wounds. They dropped their weapons and raised their hands in surrender.

Thanda spoke into his communicator. "No prisoners. Kill them, then everybody get down the hill." To Morwen, he said, "Let's go."

Another burst of firing, and the last of the would-be invaders at the Manse were dispatched. Now the three aircars equipped with heavy weapons rose into the air, while Thanda's ground troops piled into carryalls and ground cars. The vehicles roared out of the hilltop compound and onto the road leading down to New Dispensation. When they came to the first of the switchbacks, they did not turn, but slowed a little and descended straight down over the rough ground.

In the town, the starmenters had formed up into companies. Weapons drawn, they surged along the grid of streets, kicking in doors, hunting for people to chivvy along before them as human shields. But almost all the Dispers were gathered in the meeting house at the western edge of town. Kronik's constables had gone door-to-door, encouraging those who had thought to lie in bed for the holiday morning.

Now the trucks and cars came roaring down at the pirates, air cars flying above. At first, they thought it was their own allies, come to join in the round-up. But then they saw the passenger ship that had carried the assault against the Manse lift off and disappear over the northern horizon at top speed, just as the Protectors arrived, the carryalls and cars slewing to a halt, spilling out armed men in black and blue who immediately opened fire on the invaders crowded together in the streets. The slaughter began, again with no quarter.

The pirates' vehicles had been idling along behind the companies, not expecting to be needed until there were captives to carry back to the ships. Now they came under fire from the Protectors' air cars, which aimed their military-grade weapons at the still rolling ground cars and transports. Some exploded, throwing the burning corpses of their drivers to land, tumbling, on the streets. Others melted, their metals and plastics mingling with the deliquescing flesh of their occupants. The air filled with the sounds of explosions, crackling flames, screams and curses, overlaid by the shrieks and *zivv* of disorganizers and beam weapons.

Behind them, at the eastern end of town where one of Belloch's freighters had landed, the vessel lifted off, its hatches still open. Morwen, riding in Thanda's air car down to the battle, saw a man fall out of an open hatch as the ship rolled and arrowed up out of view.

One of the air car crews aimed its weapon at the fleeing ship, but Thanda spoke into his communicator, "No, we let the ships go. Companies One and Two, go to the meeting house and engage the enemy. Companies Three and Four, go south and engage. They will probably have time to flee."

"Ser," one of his senior officers said, "we could disable the ship, stop them from leaving."

"Do as I say." Thanda closed the communicator. To Morwen, he said, "You'll be worried about your parents."

"I am," she said.

"Then we'll go there."

The Protectors were climbing into their transports again. Now they accelerated toward the meeting house. The air car followed.

The distance was not great. In less than a minute, the vehicles were pulling up at the playground out front of the community hall, with its swings, and slides, and spinarounds. The pirates had come up from their ship that had landed at the western limit of Broadway and been surprised to find the building barricaded, with Kronik's constables firing at them. They had taken cover where they could find it and returned fire, waiting for reinforcements that were never going to come. Morwen could see smoke rising from the hall's wooden walls, where projac beams had missed the windows.

"At them!" Thanda ordered.

His Protectors positioned themselves behind and under the transports. Some took shelter in the doorways across the street from the meeting house. The *zivv* of beam weapons, the stuttering of slugthrowers, and the shrieks of the disorganizers from overhead mingled with the screams of the wounded.

The pirates disengaged and ran back toward their ship, harried by the weapons crews in the air cars and cut down by some of the Protectors who were proud of their marksmanship. The constabulary air car that had begun firing when the reinforcements arrived lifted off from the meeting house roof and joined the pursuit.

None of the invaders made it to the ship before it rose and flew away. Morwen looked south and saw the fourth ship climb into the sky. The sounds of weapons fire told her that it had left its assault teams on the ground to be slaughtered. The air cars that had come to the meeting house now turned their bows in that direction. She saw the crews gesturing with the excitement of being on the winning side.

The doors of the meeting house opened. Kronik emerged, with a few of his constables. "We have a couple of wounded," he said. "Nothing too serious."

Thanda spoke into his communicator, ordering his medical team to report to the hall. He told his driver to set the air car down. Morwen jumped over the side and ran to the meeting house.

"They're fine," Kronik said.

She pressed by him. Inside, the people were coming up from the basement. Dedana Llanko pushed past her and out the door. Morwen heard her say, "Hah!" and wondered if the woman's face muscles remembered how to make a smile.

But now she saw her parents and went to them. Both Chaffe and Elva showed the dark eyes and soft breathing of maunch chewers.

"Are you all right?" she said.

"Never better," said her father. "What was all that about?"

"We'll talk about it later."

But the maunch made her parents want to be out in the sunshine. They moved with the others toward the door. Outside, the Protectors were dragging the bodies of the dead toward the transports and loading them aboard.

Elva watched for a while, then said, "Well, that's not how it went last time, is it?"

Chaffe said, "Goodness, no." He took a deep delightful breath. "I feel like something tasty. Let's go home."

Arm in arm, they made their way eastward, stepping over bodies, their heads together in private conversation.

Kronik had come up beside Morwen at the top of the steps. They watched her parents go, and he said, "The Oikumeners are right. We *are* barbarians."

She said, "As we need to be."

Later in the day, a shuttle with IPCC markings made a slow descent to the Manse. Thanda and Morwen went out to meet it.

Ben Zaum stepped down, looked around, said, "I take it all went well?"

"It did at our end," Thanda said. "And at yours?"

"We brought three cruisers from the Oikumene. Antiques from museums, two of them, but still functional. They closed with Belloch's and Two Hearts's ships, disabled their engines, and boarded them."

"They are captured?" Morwen said.

"We're still sorting through them, while they're on the way back to Avente for trial. We left the ships adrift. Their owners will be traced, to see if they want to recover them."

Zaum looked around again. "Quite a set-up," he said.

"Efficient," Thanda said. "And fully accepted by the community."

"Hmm," the IPCC man said.

Thanda turned to one of his senior officers. "Bring out the pirate." To Zaum, he said, "We saved one of Two Hearts's inner circle for you. Thought he might be useful if you decide to raid his hidey-hide, free some of your citizens."

The pirate was brought out, still taped at wrist and elbow, groggy from the lingering effects of the shocker. He was bundled into the shuttle.

Zaum said, "We won't put him in with his boss." He rubbed his nose. "There will be a reward, for him, and for the bosses."

Thanda showed him a rare smile. "How about, in return for him and

— 154 —

the two pirate chiefs, our reward is that you let us go about our harm-less business unmolested."

Zaum's smile was as empty as Thanda's. "I am afraid we can't do that. The law is the law."

There was little left to be said. Zaum turned to leave, then stopped and turned back. To Morwen, he said, "Well done. If you ever want to turn weasel…"

"My life is here," she said. "I've had enough of adventuring."

The IPCC man shrugged and smiled a warmer smile than he had offered Thanda. A few moments later, his shuttle was a dwindling dot high overhead.

Morwen went to see her parents in the Manse's kitchens. The maunch would be wearing off and she was concerned they might have suffered traumatic reactions to the violence. After all, they had been through an almost identical raid — except for the different outcomes — and the morning might have brought back memories of that day, twenty-five years gone, that changed their lives forever.

But she found them in good spirits, happily at work, chopping and mixing, going back and forth from pantry to spice supplies. Elva was singing a song Morwen remembered from her childhood, Chaffe chim-ing in with harmonies in his light tenor.

Morwen thought, if she had to pick a word to describe them, it might be "sprightly." Or perhaps "exuberant." Certainly, it would not be "traumatized."

She stopped her mother in her transit of the kitchen and hugged her. Morwen was pleased to feel more flesh on her mother's frame than there used to be. Her father, too, had filled out since his eman-cipation.

"Are you all right?" she asked them.

Elva smiled the beatific smile Morwen remembered from the meet-ups. "All is well," she said, then spun away and went back to work.

Morwen thought, *We may be barbarians, but we are happy as we are.*

Life returned to normal. Some Protectors were promoted to replace the traitors. Others received recognition and commendations for their bravery in combat. Thanda told Morwen he would be sending her on a delivery to Olliphane to see about recruiting more men.

"And some women, too," she said.

He stopped and thought about it for a long moment, then said, "All right. I've prepared this advertisement to go in popular magazines like *Cosmopolis* and *Extant.*"

He handed her a piece of paper on which was printed: *Men Wanted. Seeking competent men with experience in security and investigations. Travel into and out of the Beyond. Good pay, regular hours, opportunity for advancement on merit. Apply at Mercoli Hotel, Madrigon, Olliphane, the morning of Septomese, 19.*

"I can change this?" Morwen said, "to 'Men and Women Wanted'?"

"Agreed. Macrine will place the ad. Give him the new wording. He leaves this afternoon. You will go with him on the Septomese trip to interview the prospects. Hire all that meet your standards."

"Understood. Some are likely to be weasels."

Thanda shrugged. "Likely? I would say certainly. We'll winkle them out once they get here."

Morwen went to her office and revised the advertisement, then brought it to where Lech Macrine was supervising the loading of extract into one of the small cargo vessels Thanda had bought with the proceeds from the auction at Interchange.

He put the paper in his wallet then, as Morwen went to leave, he said, "A minute, Morwen."

She turned back, to see a peculiar expression on his face.

"I know you go to the Fifthday dances sometimes," he said.

She nodded. "I do."

He cleared his throat. "I was wondering if you might like to go to one…with me."

She blinked. "I, er…"

He spoke quickly. "I know your history," he said. "We all do. How you rescued your parents and brought them here, and that was your whole life."

"Yes," she said, "but —"

"But you've done that, and it's all worked out, and now you have another life to live. After."

He stopped there, and waited for her to respond. She got over her surprise and thought of a couple of ways she could answer, then discarded them. "I'll have to think about it," she said.

There was nothing else Macrine could do but agree. He went back to work and Morwen went back to her office. She did what she had told the pilot she would do. After she had thought about it, she got her old electric-assisted bike out of the Manse's garage and drove down the hill.

It was end of shift time at the constabulary, the lights just coming on as the day eased into evening. She found Eldo Kronik in his office, tidying his desk, preparing to leave.

"Join me for dinner?" she said.

"Sure." He locked his desk drawer and stood up.

Gisby had made her shumkin and leek pie a standard at the restaurant. Morwen ordered it and found it slightly different from the recipe she had invented on the spot, but judged the change an improvement. Kronik ordered native fungi stuffed with a variety of meats, ground and seasoned.

They talked of inconsequentials, comfortable with each other. When desert — oodleberry pie with heavy cream — was finished, they ordered punge laced with a sweet liqueur. After his first sip, Kronik sighed with satisfaction.

Then Morwen said, "We should talk."

"About what?"

"About you and me."

He put down his mug. "Ah," he said.

The ensuing conversation was not long, and both participants emerged from it with satisfaction.

When the Dispers came from Tantamount, they brought with them many of the old world's customs, including the tradition of persons who were interested in a formal relationship painting the right thumbs of their intendeds a deep indigo. The next morning, Kronik and Morwen went to the store that sold decorating materials, and bought a small vial of dye. The proprietor smiled at Morwen, winked at Kronik, as the custom required.

They then went to their respective jobs, and endured the comments, some kindly meant, some frankly ribald, that blue-thumbers had had to put up with for centuries. As soon as she could, Morwen went down to the kitchens and gave her parents the news. It was well received. Chaffe and Elva thought highly of Kronik, even if he was not a man to attract affection.

"We'll get closer," her mother said. To which her father added, "Though it will take some time."

Upstairs, Thanda noticed her thumb. "Kronik?" he said.

"Kronik," she confirmed.

"Poor Macrine," Thanda said.

Macrine managed to contain his disappointment upon his return from Olliphane and his sight of Morwen's thumb. He reported that he had placed the advertisement as ordered. He then took a two-day break, which included attendance at a Fifthday dance, where he sparkled to gain the attentions of a number of young women from New Dispensation and the surrounding farms and hamlets. It was reported to Morwen by several observers that he appeared to suffer no ill effects of his affections being redirected.

The pilot's behavior was unimpeachable as they met at the Itinerator. They flew first to Hambledon's spaceport where guards from Chorestown had Belloch's captured henchman, the survivor of the kidnapping attempt, waiting in restraints. They bundled him aboard and, taking no chances, Macrine locked him in the hold among the containers of maunch extract, bound to the wall by a stout cable.

They then flew to Alphanor, where consumption of maunch extract was licit, though regulated. At the main spaceport in Avente, while Morwen covered the man with her projac, the pilot freed the pirate from the restraints and handed him a packet of SVU certificates and some identity papers forged in Thanda's establishment.

The thug flipped through the currency certificates then studied the documents. "They look real," he said.

"We keep our promises," Morwen said. "Now get out of our sight."

The man left through the forward hatch as the port's arbigers arrived to inspect the cargo. "Who was that?" the senior official said.

"Him?" said Morwen. "Just a passenger. But we suspect he is an associate of a notorious starmenter, Hacheem Belloch."

The statement startled the arbiger. She raised her wrist to her mouth and spoke into her communications bracelet, ordering the pirate's arrest. To Macrine and Morwen she said, "You can be held responsible for giving aid to known criminals."

"It won't happen again," Morwen said.

After transferring the consigned cargo to the spaceport's bonded warehouse, they proceeded to Madrigon on Olliphane, where maunch extract was outlawed. But they carried no contraband for this trip, because they meant for their presence in Madrigon to be known.

Nonetheless, when they arrived at the spaceport, they were subjected to a barrage of questions and a thorough inspection of the holds and cabins. Nothing actionable was found, and they answered the questions honestly. Finally, they were allowed to leave the port's confinement zone, though Morwen had no doubt they were followed into town.

The interviews at the Mercoli Hotel were scheduled for the following morning. Morwen and Macrine checked in — separate rooms — and she confirmed that arrangements for the meetings were in hand. She inspected the chamber, found it suitable, then ate dinner in her room and went to bed.

In the morning, she arrived at the interview room to find twenty-seven applicants, including six women, waiting for Macrine and her. They gave each candidate a number and called them in, one at a time.

To begin with, she and Macrine examined qualifications and employment histories while taking a good look at the physical condition of each would-be Protector. After an hour and a half, they had winnowed the initial group down to sixteen men and five women who seemed to fit the requirements.

They then began to interview the individual applicants in depth. By lunch time, they had selected seven of the men and three of the women to whom they would make offers of a probationary employment. They had rejected one of the women and four of the men in the initial crowd, and still had to make up their minds about the remaining six. They sent them all away, with a promise to let them know the decisions the next day.

They talked it over during lunch. Macrine was of the opinion that two of the undecideds could be IPCC weasels, and he had doubts about one of the men they had already chosen.

"We'll let Thanda and his interrogators deal with them," Morwen said. "Our job is to bring home a decent pool of candidates."

They went back to the interview room and consulted the resumes and references again, comparing the documents with their own notes as to the various impressions the applicants had made. By mid afternoon, they had decided against two of the six maybes. That left them with ten men and four women who qualified for a probationary offer.

They packed up their papers and prepared to leave the interview room. At that point the door opened and five men entered. Each wore the uniform and insignia of the IPCC. All were armed. And one of them was Ben Zaum.

He greeted them by name. Then he said, "I have a detention order for each of you. I would appreciate it if you did not make a fuss."

Chapter Nine

Morwen and Macrine were taken to a nondescript building, separated, and placed in different interrogation rooms. Morwen wondered if there was any meaning to place on the fact that they had not been restrained. She walked around the small space for a while, to take the tension-induced stiffness out of her muscles, then sat in a chair at the table and waited. From time to time, she glanced at the lens mounted in one corner where the walls met the ceiling. The last time, she raised her eyebrows and her hands in a gesture that said, *Let's get on with it.*

A short time later, Ben Zaum entered the room and sat opposite her. He opened a folder and affected to read what was written on the top page of a file.

"There was no contraband on our ship," she said, keeping her tone mild. "On what grounds are you detaining us?"

He pretended to read to the end of a paragraph then looked at her. "You're a known associate of a prominent criminal from the Beyond. I can hold you for three days, and extend for three more."

"What prominent criminal?" Morwen said.

"A couple, actually. Jerz Thanda, of course, since you are his second in command."

"And the other?"

Zaum smiled. "The pirate, Hacheem Belloch."

Morwen snorted. "You're joking. I am — I was — a *victim* of Belloch's."

"We can argue semantics," Zaum said. "We have three days to kill."

Morwen had gotten over her surprise. "Besides, you've got the *fagreen* in custody." She watched his carefully controlled expression, then grew concerned. "Don't you?"

Zaum looked at the opposite wall. "Things did not go as planned. Belloch was aboard the freighter that landed on the east side of town. As soon as he saw his men ambushed, he ordered it aloft, but before it left the atmosphere he got into an air car and flew to Hambledon spaceport.

"There, he commandeered a small space ship, forcing its owner at gunpoint to take him offworld. Our sources at Boregore tell us that he did not return to Blatcher's World."

Now he looked meaningfully at Morwen, and said, "Before he used the air car to depart from the freighter, he threw Sheleen Two Hearts to his death from an open hatch. We have reason to believe Belloch somehow acquired the astrogation vectors that would lead him to an unnamed world. He has gone there to hide out."

Morwen understood. Hacheem had gone to the nameless, hidden world Two Hearts had bought at Interchange. He would hide out there and plot his return to piracy. Revenge against those who had thwarted his raid on New Dispensation would be a high and permanent item on his agenda.

"And you think," she said, "that I know where that world is. But I don't."

She recounted the events at Interchange, then added, "I saw three long lines of numbers and letters. I don't remember them."

Zaum raised a hand to stop her. "Perhaps you do," he said, then kept the hand up to reject her denial. He turned toward the device in the corner and said, "Send him in."

The door opened and a small man with thinning hair and an abstracted expression came into the room. He wore the robe and insignia, the one tattered and the other unpolished, of a scholar of the Institute headquartered on Earth. Zaum waved him to a seat beside him.

"This is Glaub Ishmil," he said, "from the Institute."

The newcomer had a voice as dry as an ancient manuscript. "Rank 74."

Morwen had recognized the costume — it was frequently parodied in satirical cartoons — but she had grown up knowing little of the Institute. Its members were rare in the Beyond, where they were generally treated the same as weasels, on the general understanding that the less the Oikumene knew about the denizens of the Beyond, the better. And their abstruse activities were far from the daily lives of a barbarian pirate or his slaves.

Zaum said, "Ser Ishmil's area of interest is human mentation, with a particular focus on memory. He has developed a serum that sharpens recollections remarkably."

"I don't want my mentation sharpened," Morwen said. "I'm satisfied with it the way it is, and I have plenty of memories I would just as soon be rid of."

"Then you'll have ample time to shed those memories while you're in indefinite detention."

"On what grounds?"

"Obstructing an investigation."

Morwen felt aggrieved. "You could not do this to me if I were a citizen of an Oikumene world."

"Quite right," said the IPCC agent. "But you're not. You're a captured Beyonder. A known criminal."

A barbarian, thought Morwen.

It was two days before Morwen felt she was fully recovered from the effects of the serum. They had blindfolded her before tipping the little vial of bitter-tasting liquid over her lips. As soon as the compound began to work, it was as if her head had filled with bright light. At first, she saw a whirling kaleidoscope of scenes, all arrayed as if she were looking into a myriad tiny rooms. As soon as she focused on one, it filled her inner vision, and she was seeing some moment that had passed before her eyes.

There seemed no plan or system of organization. Sights from her early childhood were placed beside events from last year. Harrowing moments were jostled up against the times of pure boredom that were part of every slave's life. And every tiny scene remained frozen and still, until she willed it to play out; then she had sound and motion and even the trace of scent and warmth.

The Institute man's voice came to her in the darkness. "The first moment you placed the encrypted bead in a reader and said the password."

As soon as he said it, the image came into her head. She saw the reader, her hand withdrawing from placing the orb, the screen appearing in the air before her.

"Follow it," said the voice.

She did, and the three strings of numbers, each several digits long, came to life before her. "Freeze it and read it," said the voice.

The drug gave her no choice. She read the three vectors aloud, then upon instruction, read them again.

"Good," said another voice. She recognized it as Zaum's. "Feed that into the navigator and let's be on our way."

The blindfold remained in place. She had been seated in a chair, and now the chair began to move. She was wheeled forward half a minute, then turned to the right. Her stomach told her she was in an ascendor, going up. Then more travel, a couple of more turns, and she stopped.

Zaum's voice again. "Reach out and you will feel a bunk. Lie on it and relax. Ser Ishmil says that the serum will be a while wearing off. Best if you remain still and quiet in the dark until then. Trying to use your vision while your mind is throwing up memories…well, it can lead to stumbles and falls.

"Just wait in the cabin with the lights out until you're right again."

He left her then and she heard the lock on the door engage — left her with a lifetime of memories, each in its own little box, as if she faced a wall of tiny compartments, infinitely high and infinitely wide. She could not help focusing on this one or that, in which case it leapt to prominence and began to play out.

She relaxed as best she could and wished for sleep, but the serum promoted wakefulness. She was left with no choice but to experience her whole life in one snippet after another. She wondered if there was truth to the myth that, at the moment of death, a person's life flashed before their eyes, and Ishmil had somehow discovered a way to unlock that capability. If so, she soon concluded, he ought to be dipped in lard and roasted over a slow fire.

Within her mind, there was nowhere to look where she did not encounter an image, and as soon as she noticed it, that image came to life. Morwen endured the process inertly for a while, until she was forced to conclude that most of her life had been a waste. It had been lived at the orders of a brutal tyrant who cared nothing for her. She was to bring his wants to him, without delay. His will would send her scurrying back and forth, from kitchen to parlor, or out to wherever he might be on the estate, if he fancied a snack while he was about his piratical affairs.

She called up a few such images and saw, again, his complete disregard for her, for any of his slaves. Belloch's sexual proclivities ran to exquisite courtesans, trained in the most arcane of erotic arts. His slaves might as well have been domesticated animals; indeed, they were commonly referred to by Belloch and his overseer, Vilch, as "livestock."

The helpless hate she had often felt for him, and which had faded during the days since she had won her freedom and her parents', came back. The idea that he had escaped retribution raised a black anger in her. Now she was not resentful that the Institute scholar had created this strange effect within her mind. If her present discomfort led to the undoing of Hacheem Belloch, then it was no discomfort at all.

So she lay, brooding on her pointless past, thinking of all the other, happier experiences that might have been hers had not the Demon Princes descended on Mount Pleasant. And she let the rage fill her. It was better than the emptiness that the helplessness of slavery had imposed upon her.

Eventually, she slept. When she woke, the endless wall of tiny images was still there. But its brightness had faded, its colors dulled. She found she could let her inner gaze roam over the array and, if she stopped, it did not automatically go into action. And when she did call up a memory, it lacked the presence that had infused the experiences when the serum was fresh in her veins.

Finally, over the course of an hour or so, the pictures faded to nothing. Morwen groped around the head of the bunk, found the control that worked the lumen, and filled the cabin with light. There was an ablutory behind a sliding door. She refreshed herself then sat on the bunk until she was sure of her state of mind.

Then she pushed the stud that activated the communicator set into the wall. A moment later, Zaum's voice said, "All better?"

"Much."

"I'll send someone to bring you."

• • •

The ship was larger than any Morwen had ever been on, with multiple decks. She had heard of big passenger liners that plied between the grand worlds of the Oikumene, but this vessel showed no signs of the luxury and excess she associated with the civilization on the other side of the Pale. It was functional, stark, a warship from a bygone age.

A woman in an Ipsy uniform took her to a room where Zaum waited with a handful of other agents, grouped around a long table with rounded ends. All had insignia of rank on their collars and cuffs. Zaum did not bother to introduce her, but waved her to a seat beside him.

He looked her over, then said, "No lingering effects?"

She decided to be frank with him. "I was once again caused to relive my years of slavery. It was not a happy experience."

She did not tell him that some of the memories had revived her childhood terror at the sight of Hacheem Belloch. She preferred to focus on the rage.

He let his hands express regret. "Necessity," he said. "Belloch must be paid out for his crimes."

"On that, we agree," Morwen said. "Indeed, I would like to be there for the paying."

"With any luck, that will happen soon." He told the ship to light up a screen that took up most of one wall beyond the end of the table. They saw the strangeness that surrounded the vessel while the Jarnell drive was active. After a short while, the lights and fluxes fell away and they were back in normal space, facing the great gas cloud. Then they entered it.

It took less time than Morwen remembered before they came out into the rift with its white dwarf blazing like a pinprick pushed through the dark to some great light beyond. The dead planets hung in their orbits, and the nameless world showed itself.

"Scan," Zaum said into a bracelet on his wrist.

Moments later, a disembodied voice spoke from nearby. "Ship located. On the prominence. Some kind of building under construction."

"People?"

"One for sure, maybe two. We'll know better when we're closer."

Zaum ordered the macroscope scan transferred to the screen before them. That was when Morwen learned the room they were in was called the wardroom. It was another ancient term, like "cockpit," whose origin was lost in the mists of time.

An image swam into being: the height she remembered from the initial visit; a compact yacht parked on it; a partially constructed dome made of prefabricated triangles that could be interlocked. More of the three-sided panels were stacked outside the ship.

"Weapons?" Zaum said.

"None heavy."

"Let's be careful," the IPCC man said. "Arm all systems, stand to."

A klaxon sounded, three bleats. Morwen heard the sounds of running feet, doors slamming closed. "Ready for action," said the voice.

"Prepare to disable that ship if it tries to leave," Zaum said.

"Targeted," came the reply.

"And here we go," said Zaum.

Morwen found herself leaning forward, staring at the screen as she had recently stared at her own memories. She wanted to see Belloch. Wanted to see him try to run. At the same time, a child's terror was pushing through her anger, gibbering at her from somewhere at the edges of her mind. She fought it, but found herself strung between the two extremes of emotion.

The serum was still affecting her, she realized. She would have to fight the lingering effects.

The ship guided itself down to where it cruised barely above the flat, lichen-covered surface, over the horizon from the prominence on which the space yacht and the half-built dome waited. It then approached silently, as warships — even ancient ones — were designed to do.

Zaum and three of his officers armed themselves with projacs and went down to one of the sally ports, where an armored, multi-person air car waited. Morwen, with no one to tell her different, followed them. When Zaum raised the canopy to board the vehicle, she took a seat.

He frowned at her, but she returned him as determined a glare as she could muster, until he shrugged and indicated a seat at the rear of the craft. She moved, then they waited, canopy closed and drive idling, until the port opened.

The ship was hovering below the top of the precipice, keeping out of view of anyone there. The air car slipped out, then moved along the face of the cliff until it was able to rise silently to where the half-built dome was sited. It moved until it was positioned out of sight behind the yacht, and hovered a handsbreadth above the flat surface. The four IPCC agents clambered out, weapons drawn. They arrayed themselves between the yacht and the dome and advanced steadily.

Morwen followed them. She found herself trembling, partly from fear, partly from anger. She was thinking, *This is the moment you thought would never come.* She wished they had given her back her projac. She imagined aiming at the master — that was the old word that came stealing into her mind — and the tremors increased.

Zaum and his men moved silently. This side of the dome was mostly constructed, though there was a doorway that lacked a door. Triangular panels were stacked up outside and now that Morwen focused on the details of the scene, she saw a coiled whip hanging on a nail beside the doorway.

She knew that whip, had seen it wielded. Fashioned from the braided hide of some dark-skinned beast, tipped with three iron points, it was Hacheem's symbol of power. He often carried it. The sight of it sent a chilling shock through Morwen. The first time she had seen it used, she had been a little girl. The victim was a woman who had been kind to her. Morwen had had nightmares for months.

Find the rage, she told herself. *It will smother the fear.*

Her thoughts were cut off as she heard activity inside the dome. Then a figure appeared in the doorway, stooping to reach for a panel. He froze at the sight of the IPCC agents, his face registering almost comical surprise.

He was not Hacheem Belloch. He was a man older than his middle years, dressed in clothes of soft fabric, with puffed sleeves and billowing pantaloons, his feet in brocaded slippers — just what a prosperous retiree might wear while lounging in the saloon of his own yacht. And still wearing them after being boarded by a vicious, whip-wielding pirate who forced him to fly to this desolate nowhere, then put him to work.

Wordlessly, Zaum beckoned to the man to come out. But the shock was too great. The victim remained frozen. Morwen heard a sharp inquiry from within the dome. She recognized the voice and the tone, and flinched from habit. She was glad she was behind Zaum and the others so they did not see her ingrained response.

A shape appeared behind the forced laborer. The police agents raised their weapons, but too late. The man was jerked backward into the dome, only to emerge moments later with Belloch's arm across his throat and a projac aimed at his head.

"Lower your weapons, or I boil his brains," the pirate said.

"Do that," said Zaum, "and we cut you down."

"Out of my way," Belloch ordered. He pushed his hostage forward a step, the man's face white with fear. It hadn't taken long, Morwen thought, for the master to do what he was best at: reducing another human being to a state of abject terror.

The scene remained motionless for several moments, then Zaum told his men to stand aside. "We'll pursue," he said. "We can disable your engines and board you in space."

"And if you do," Belloch said, "you'll enter a ship to find this fellow carved into pieces."

Morwen saw Zaum consider the option, then reject it. "Your men are dead," he said. "When we raid your hidey-hide, who will defend you?"

Belloch grinned. "I'd be a poor pirate if I didn't have more than one base. And if I couldn't raise a new company of bravos. I'll see you when I come."

He pushed the yacht owner through the IPCC line. "And maybe, in the meantime, I'll send someone to visit your families."

Zaum's face was grim. He half-raised his projac. But Belloch cocked his head and gave him a mocking smile, and the colonel-investigator subsided.

Now the pirate came face to face with Morwen and, after a moment, recognized her. "Kitchen girl," he said. "We meet again. Wonderful."

Morwen's blood turned cold in her veins. Her breath came short.

Hacheem said, "Go to the dome and fetch my whip."

She instinctively began to obey the order, then stopped. But then she saw outrage flare in her former master's face and the word "former" lost all meaning. On legs that felt leaden, she passed through the IPCC agents, reached the dome, and plucked the coiled whip from its hook. Then she plodded back to Belloch. Zaum put out a hand to stop her, but she shook him off.

The pirate had turned his hostage and now they were backing toward the yacht. "Come along, kitchen girl," he said. "I'll teach you some new tricks."

She reached him and he said, "Get aboard. Be ready to close the hatch on my command."

Her will had deserted her. Her rage was smothered by the years of childhood training, backed by a child's fear, and now brought back by the Institute scholar's memory-inducing drug. *I'm no barbarian,* she thought. *I'm just a barbarian's slave.*

A series of images came to her inner vision: scenes of degradation and despair, of nights begun in tears and ended in nightmares. She felt helpless, futile, tiny.

She reached the yacht's open hatch. It was dark and unlit inside, the ship's systems powered down to save its energy supplies. She contemplated stepping into that darkness and all that that one step would mean to her.

She turned and saw Belloch backing toward her, his weapon at the stolen man's head, his posture and movements bespeaking great confidence in his mastery of the situation. Beyond them, the IPCC agents stood glum and silent.

And then a new vision came to her: from the time in the meeting house, after she chewed the maunch. She remembered the light, the faces looking back at her, the sense of limitless life that infused her with every ecstatic breath. The voice from within, filling her with power.

Don't think, that voice now spoke in her mind. *Just do. All shall be well.*

Morwen did not pause to think or feel. She took one step toward Hacheem Belloch, dropped the loop of the whip over his head, and pulled it tight about his neck, yanking him back toward her.

He lost his balance for a moment, letting go of the hostage, trying instead to turn within the whip's grip and bring the projac to bear upon her. But she yanked hard again, at the same time swinging him sideways along the yacht's hull, toward its bow that hung over the edge of the precipice.

He stumbled again, tried to right himself, seeking to get the beam pistol aimed over his shoulder to shoot her. But now she had him where she wanted him. Space was limited atop the cliff. The yacht was parked with its nose over the edge, the yawning drop only a step away.

She heard footsteps behind her: Zaum and his three agents rushing to seize the moment.

No, she thought. *All shall be well.* She knew with complete certainty what was about to happen.

She let go of the whip. Released, Belloch spun to face her, his features animated by wild glee. But even as the projac came down to bear on her, he was adjusting his stance to steady himself. One foot moved backward, the heel touching the very lip of the precipice.

She saw his smile of triumph. Zaum and the IPCC agents had stopped behind her, frozen again by Belloch's unspoken threat to kill her. The pirate beckoned her with the projac. "Into the ship, kitchen girl."

And then the friable rock beneath his heel crumbled and gave way. Belloch teetered on the edge, drawn backward. His free hand reached out to Morwen in an instinctive gesture.

She folded her arms across her chest, and smiled.

More rock broke beneath his foot. He tried to point the weapon at her, but he was toppling backward like a felled tree. In a moment, he was gone.

The antique warship hovered just below the cliff's edge. She heard him strike its upper hull. She dropped to hands and knees and moved forward, just in time to see him scrabbling at the ship's smoothly polished surface, dropping the beam pistol in a desperate search for something to grip.

But he found nothing. He slid, slowly, then with increasing speed, down the curved hull of the vessel. And now he was falling. His scream was more rage than terror, Morwen thought, and it faded with the great distance to the rocks below. She saw him strike, a tiny dot.

And that, she told herself, *is that.*

• • •

They let her keep the whip. She put it in a drawer in the cabin they assigned her. From time to time, she would open the drawer to regard the object and wonder at the mixed emotions the sight of it inevitably raised in her. She decided she would show it to Kronik, but not to her parents. Or at least not until they had chewed the maunch a few more times.

The travel time back to the Oikumene stretched into several days. Morwen had little in common with the Ipsy crew. She took her meals in her cabin and avoided contact with them. Zaum had assured her that, upon their return to Olliphane, she would be released with no further proceedings against her. Thanda's ship had been freed from impound, and Lech Macrine would be waiting to take her home to New Dispensation.

"There are no guarantees, however, if you make future runs with maunch or its extract to worlds where it is prohibited," he added. "The law is the law, and will be enforced."

She shrugged. "I may reorder my plans," she said. "It seems I am a work in progress."

Glaub Ishmil came to see her. He sat in a chair in her cabin, refused a mug of punge from the dispenser, and contemplated her as if she were a specimen of an unusual beast in a menagerie. After some time, he said, "I understand you are a maunch-eater."

"I've used it twice," she said.

"And you believe it is of benefit to you?"

"I know it has been."

Ishmil made a thoughtful noise. "I am interested in its properties, especially its effects on aberrant societies."

"Aberrant?" she said.

"Those beyond the Pale," he said, "where the rule of law is, shall we say, more of an abstraction than an everyday reality."

Morwen wasn't sure how to respond.

"It is difficult," the Institute scholar said, when no response was forthcoming, "to study such phenomena in the field. Our people must travel incognito, at a risk of being taken up by the Deweaseling Corps."

Morwen signaled her agreement. "A great deal of suspicion is directed at inquisitive outsiders."

"Would you — you, personally — be averse to assisting in such research?" Ishmil said.

"Me? You don't mean would I enroll at the Institute?"

That brought a bark of laughter, followed by an apology. "No, I meant would you be willing to be contacted by one of our people on your home world and answer some questions?"

Morwen gave it some thought. "If it did not compromise my existing loyalties," she said. "When do you think you might be able to send someone to Providence?"

"Oh," said Ishmil, "we already have people there. I'll let them know you're amenable to an interview."

She rendezvoused with Macrine at a hotel near the spaceport at Madrigon on Olliphane. They had cut the pilot loose soon after he was taken, but told him he would have to wait for her to return and for their ship to be released. He had considered it a vacation, although Madrigon — like all of Olliphane — was organized around several heavy industries. Tourists were not expected, nor much catered for.

In her absence, he had kept in contact with the successful applicants for probationary enrollment in the Protectors. Now they rounded them up and took them aboard the freighter. They lifted off, Macrine set the controls, and they engaged the intersplit drive as soon as they achieved the minimum distance from the planet.

The trip was not long, and much of Morwen's time was taken up answering the recruits' questions about Providence, New Dispensation, and the duties they would be trained for. She answered as best she could, straddling a judicious line between too little information and too much.

When they touched down outside the Manse, she handed off the fourteen to Subcommander Gwllero and went to her office. Here she hid Hacheem Belloch's whip in a cupboard, then went to the kitchens to visit her parents. She did not tell them what had happened with her. She would let that information out in small pieces.

But she did go immediately after to the constabulary, where she had a long talk with Eldo Kronik. They agreed on several matters of importance, and set a schedule for the steps to follow.

"We are compatible in most of the ways that matter," she concluded at the end of their conversation. "But there is the issue of intimacy."

Kronik said, "There is no better way to determine compatibility than a full field test."

"Agreed," said Morwen. "Come to my house. I will make dinner and we will conduct the test."

That evening, they did so. Next morning, both declared the test a resounding success.

They went to the next Fifthday dance as a couple. The afternoon before, Kronik and Morwen had painted each other's left thumbs a bright scarlet, signaling that they had moved from being "intendeds" to the state of formal betrothal. Congratulations came from all sides.

They danced a few parades and terpsichords, then Kronik went to get them cooling sherbets while Morwen stepped out onto the little landing beyond the hall's side door. A moment later, someone came and stood beside her.

"Eldo?" she said when he did not speak.

But it was not her betrothed. Yet it was a familiar face. "Is this a good time to speak?" said Tosh Hubbley.

"As good as any," she replied.

He spoke softly. "Glaub Ishmil, Rank 74, said you were amenable to talking about maunch."

"You're with the Institute?" she said.

"I am, but obviously I would prefer not to be known as such to your employer. At least not yet."

Morwen's brow contracted. "I thought you were born and bred on Providence."

"The infant Tosh Hubbley died on the journey from Worstead to Hambledon. His parents had been negligent. Fearing repercussions, they did not report the death but buried the child beside the trail. They themselves took the secret to their graves. When I arrived on Providence, I searched the records and secured the child's identity. I then took work as a sales representative, which allowed me to visit many places and make observations."

"Remarkable," said Morwen. "But whatever you have to say, you had better say it before my fiancé arrives."

Hubbley told her there was no hurry. "Maddie has engaged him in conversation."

The surprises kept piling up, Morwen thought. "Maddie is one of you?"

"A crossroads hotel with a tavern is an excellent place to acquire information. Also it makes a fine meeting point for passing on clandestine messages."

Morwen spoke a mild profanity. "Tell me what you want," she said.

"The Institute has been following the spread of maunch use and calculating its effects in the Beyond. We have come to the conclusion that it is what we call a 'good thing'."

"Good how?" Morwen said.

"There are technical descriptions, but in lay terms, it makes people less inclined to tear at each other like wild beasts. It also augments the collaborative impulse."

"That does sound like a 'good thing'."

The Institute thinks in terms of centuries, Hubbley told her. One of its longer-term goals was to create a cohesive civilization that extended the length of the galactic arm.

"An empire?" she said.

Hubbley snorted. "Never," he said. "Rather an array of autonomous worlds, ten thousand of them, each pursuing its own destiny, but none seeking to oppress another. We call it the Gaean Reach."

"It has a ring to it," Morwen said.

Jerz Thanda, in his pursuit of profit, had already unknowingly begun the work. Hubbley told her that the Institute was prepared to offer him information on other worlds that would be receptive to the introduction of maunch, with or without the religious trappings.

Morwen chuckled. "You would be Thanda's market research department."

"In effect."

She thought about it, came to a decision. "I will talk to him about it."

"No names," Hubbley said.

"I will lay the proposal at Ishmil's door."

"A wise decision. You may tell Maddie anything you want me to hear."

With that, Hubbley descended the steps and disappeared into the darkness.

Kronik came out, bearing two paper cups of sherbet. "That girl from the hotel wanted to tell me about something, though it made no sense. I think she's scatter brained. I hope you were not bored."

"Not at all," Morwen said, accepting her sherbet. "I don't expect to be bored ever again."

Eldo Kronik took that as a compliment.

Epilogue

Time passed, New Dispensation continued to flourish, and Morwen Sabine and Eldo Kronik were happy in their new life in a house they bought together. She gradually brought Jerz Thanda around to the idea of using the Institute's assistance to expand the maunch extract business, and when that proved to be beneficial to the enterprise, her employer cut her in for one per cent of the profits.

He also improved her access to intelligence, routinely including her in the weekly sessions during which his operatives brought home information acquired during their trips into the Oikumene and to other worlds of the Beyond. It was at one of these meetings that Lech Macrine made a startling announcement.

"Interchange has gone out of business," the pilot said.

Thanda actually let his impassive face show surprise. "What? How?"

"A man calling himself Howard Wall managed to pass ten billion SVU into their system, rescinding the fees of a female guest who was the object of Kokor Hekkus's desire. He walked out with her and a draft on the Interplanetary Bank on Sasani."

Macrine paused to shake his head in wonder and admiration, then continued, "But the ten billion certificates were counterfeit — don't ask me how they fooled the fake meter — and soon they faded into just so many pieces of blank paper. Interchange was instantly bankrupt and could no longer meet its obligations to the bank, which seized all its assets and shut it down."

"What happened to the 'guests'?" Morwen said.

"The bank had no interest in running a ransom and slave auction business," the pilot said. "They used the remaining funds in Interchange's accounts to charter a liner and ship them all back to the Oikumene."

Thanda said, "Amazing. I'd like to meet this Howard Wall and hear how he managed to fool the fake meter. It's never been done before."

He paused, thinking, and added, "Then I would kill him so that I never have to worry about any customer slipping me a bag of dud SVU certificates."

"It's doubtful you ever will," said Macrine. "Everybody from the IPCC to the Deweaseling Corps is looking for him, but he has vanished from sight. There is a rumor he has gone searching for a mythical planet far down the galactic arm."

Thanda grunted. "Probably the best place for him if he has upset Kokor Hekkus's plans. I would never want to be on the agenda of the Demon Prince they call 'the killing machine'."

Morwen and the rest of Thanda's crew concurred with their boss's sentiment. Then the meeting moved on to other business.

END

•

Colophon

This book was printed using 11,5 pt Adobe Arno Pro as the primary
text font, with NeutraFace used for titles.

Special thanks to Steve Sherman.

Book composition & Typesetting: Joel Anderson
Typographic design: Howard Kistler
Jacket blurb: Matthew Hughes
Management: John Vance, Koen Vyverman

Made in the USA
Columbia, SC
06 August 2021

43108835R00112